WRITERS REPUBLIC

Flaunting that *Mistress*

Jerraine Letitia Fuller

WRITERS REPUBLIC L.L.C.
515 Summit Ave. Unit R1
Union City, NJ 07087, USA

Website: *www.writersrepublic.com*
Hotline: *1-877-656-6838*
Email: *info@writersrepublic.com*

Ordering Information:
Quantity sales. Special discounts are available on quantity purchases by corporations, associations, and others. For details, contact the publisher at the address above.

Library of Congress Control Number: 2021918228
ISBN-13: 978-1-63728-783-5 [Paperback Edition]
978-1-63728-784-2 [Digital Edition]

Rev. date: 09/10/2021

I would first like to thank my Lord and Savior for making this possible. Lord, I thank you. I also would like to thank my wonderful husband who supports me with everything that I choose to do. He has been so wonderful and has been my confidant through this amazing journey. I also would like to thank my two children for being so proud of their mother making her passion come true. I would like to also think my friends and coworkers for their support. But most of all, I want to give thanks to the most incredible woman in the world, my mother. She had told me up until the day she passed that I am capable of doing anything that I want to in life. I have a gift, and I need to use it. So I dedicate this new beginning as being an author to her. "I did it, Mommy."

Part 1

Catrina Jones (who went by Trina) was a beautiful caramel Blasian with a body to die for. Trina was twenty-four years old getting her grind on, working to open her shoe and clothing store. She was living home with her parents and brother but was trying hard to move out on her own. She had taken all the money from her grandfather's inheritance and put it into her business. But every time she thought she was moving forward, something would always happen.

She drives a 2000 Honda that would always break down on her, but on one cold winter day, she had had enough. Trina was on the side of the road in the freezing cold. She called her father to come help her. She told her father, "Please hurry up. It's cold, Daddy. I'm too cute to freeze in the cold alone."

Her father is part Asian and African American, fifty-four years old, tall, and caramel just like his daughter. Women went crazy over Billy. They called him Billy, short for William.

He said to Trina, "Just sit still, I'm coming." He was straight-up, tell-it-like-it-is guy. "I told you to trade that damn piece of shit in a year ago. Hardheaded like Lena."

"Just hurry, Daddy. It's gettin' dark, and someone might get your daughter!"

"Trina, I been praying someone take you off my hands."

She laughed.

"Trina, I'm coming. I'm ten minutes away."

"Okay, my flashers are on. I'm about a mile from my store." She hung up.

Trina was sitting there cold and rubbing her hands together when a big black GMC truck with tinted windows pulled over and backed up in front of her car.

She said, "*Shit!*"

The driver, dressed in a suit, got out. He was tall with gray eyes, bow legs, and curly hair. His name's Kenneth Brown, a twenty-five-year-old. Trina went to school with him. He was a real woman's man. Trina always liked him in school but always turned him down when he asked her out.

Kenneth had his own business (clothing and shoe line) and an investor in the stock market.

Trina put her window down.

"Hello, pretty lady," he said, smiling.

"Hi, Kenneth!"

"Won't start?"

"No, my dad's on his way."

"Okay. You look cold. Come sit in the truck and get warm."

"No, I'm fine."

"Trina, you're shaking." He opened her door. "Come on, I promise I won't bite."

She got her purse.

He opened the truck door, and she got in with his help.

"Kenneth, stop looking at my ass."

"I'm not." He smiled. He closed the door, then turned the lights off in her car. "You don't want your battery to die." He handed Trina her keys.

"Thanks," she said.

He turned the heat up and gave her his hot chai tea. "Here, drink it."

"No, I'm fine."

"I just got it. Please drink it, Trina."

She took it from him and drank some. "Thank you, it tastes good."

"So where you coming from, Trina?"

"My store. I'm trying to open by next month."

"Oh, okay, the spot that I tried to get but homeboy leased to you?"

"Sorry," she said, smiling. "Kenneth, you have enough around here. Let a sister get something, damn!"

"You got that, Trina. So what can you do for me?"

Trina said, "*What!*"

"Hold up. Chill, short stuff," he said. "You ready to go off. Let me explain first."

"Start explaining, Kenneth."

"Let me take you out."

"Why?" she asked.

"Because you are drinking my damn chai tea, woman."

She burst out laughing. "Where, Kenneth?"

"Any place you want to go."

Trina said, "Okay, Friday night the club. You pick me up, and tell all your lil' bitches don't fuck with me. I'm not the one."

"Yes, ma'am!"

"And do you smile at everything, Kenneth?"

"No, just at you."

"Whatever!"

"Looks like your father…"

"Yes, and my uncle."

Kenneth got out and went around, helping Trina out of the truck.

Trina's dad said, "Kenneth."

"Yes, sir," he replied.

"Thanks for sitting with Trina."

"Anytime."

"Your keys, baby girl," said her uncle Willis, her dad's brother.

Her uncle was quiet, stayed to himself, worked hard, and was crazy about his niece. He would do anything for her, and she would do anything for him as well. She told him, "One day, Uncle Willis, I'm going to buy a tow company for you and Daddy."

"Trina," he said, "baby girl, you need a new car."

"All my money's tied up right now."

"We'll work it out. But for now, you can drive my car to get around."

"Thank you," Trina said. She stood and watched them put her car on the tow truck.

Kenneth said, "Let me take you home." He walked over and told her father and uncle he would take Trina home.

"Trina, you okay with that?"

"Yes," she replied.

"Call me."

"I will, Daddy."

He opened the door, and she got in. Then he pulled off, blowing the horn.

"Have you eaten yet?"

"No, not since this morning."

He pulled into the Soul Food Spot. He said, "What now, Trina?"

"What do you want, Kenneth? You're being too nice."

"Oh my god, I just want to sit down and eat. What kind of dudes you are used to dealing with?"

"Players like you."

"Whatever. You coming or what?"

She got out.

"The short ones always talk a lot of trash."

He opened the door, and they both went inside. A few of his so-called female friends were sitting inside having dinner. He paid for two.

"Trina, come on."

They sat down and ordered drinks. Trina stood up and took her coat off.

"Lawdy, Lawdy, Lawdy," he said. "Trina, your mama need to stop feeding you those greens, girl, *damn*...phat to death!"

"Can we go get our food, please, so I can go home."

"Sure, short stuff."

Kenneth spoke to the ladies, particularly Nikki, who he was seeing every now then. Nikki's few years older, has brown skin, tall, and skinny. Thought she was the shit. She told Kenneth to call her later so she could come over. She always wanted to be seen.

"Nikki, don't do that," he said. "You know what type of party we got going on. Now go sit down with your sisters and stop trying to show your ass."

Trina smiled and kept walking.

Nikki looked at Trina and said, "What the fuck is so funny?"

Trina asked, "Are you talking to me?"

"Yeah, I'm talking to you.

"First of all, you're funny, making an ass of yourself. I'm not doing your man or any other woman's man in here. But if I wanted your man, I would get your man, so back the fuck up. I'll tear you a new asshole trick." Trina walked away, fixing her plate.

Kenneth said, "Nikki, chill, damn! I don't belong to you. I'll see you when I see you, and it's not tonight." He fixed his plate and walked to the table.

Trina's dad was calling her phone. She answered, "Hey, Daddy. I'm sorry, I'm at the Soul Food Spot. I'll be home soon."

"Your mom called, saying you didn't make it home and some dude been calling the house all day."

"Who, Daddy?" Trina asked.

"Mitchell."

"Daddy tell him don't call the house anymore. I don't have time for him."

Mitchell Lee, the lawyer, is a twenty-seven-year-old Blasian brother. He is short, sexy, light skin, with wavy hair, and married to a woman older than him. He took Trina out a few times until she saw him with his wife. So she ended the friendship with him, but he still kept calling her.

"Daddy, I gotta go. My food's getting cold," she said.

Kenneth asked, "Boyfriend problems?"

"No, not at all," Trina told him. "Look, I'm not into drama, so let's not do Friday?"

"Ms. Jones, we doing Friday, so don't punk out now." He lifted his glass for a toast. "To new beginnings, Trina."

He ate off her plate, and Trina said, "No, you don't."

"You can have some of my food, Trina."

"No, thanks. I'm finished."

"Okay." He pulled money out and put a tip on the table. "Let's go, short stuff." He helped her into her coat, and they left.

Nikki watched, saying, "Check this shit out! He never opened my door up. She was hot!"

Cleo, Kenneth's best friend since elementary school, pulled up. He stood about six foot seven, three hundred pounds, nice as can be, and would help you if needed. People always said Kenneth and Cleo was into drugs, but if they were, they kept it on the down low.

Cleo put the window down. "Bro, who's that?"

Kenneth smiled, saying, "It's Trina."

"No, it's not!" He got out, opening the door.

Trina said, "Hello, Cleo, how are you?"

"I'm good now that I see you around."

"Have a good one, I'll holla at you, Cleo," Trina said.

Kenneth stood outside the truck, talking to Cleo for a few, then they hugged and did their lil' handshake.

Kenneth got in the truck and said, "Home, right?"

"Yes, please," replied Trina.

"You can come keep me company tonight."

"No, thanks, Kenneth."

"Well, left or right turn?"

"Now you know where I live at, don't play."

"Oh yeah, it's a left."

*****

Smiling, he put the truck in Park and got out.

Trina's brother was standing out front with his friend, smoking.

Kenneth said, "Hey, what's up, Timmy."

As Trina got out, Kenneth handed her his card. "If you need a ride to or from work or just want to talk to me. But until Friday, stay warm."

"I will, and thanks again, Kenneth," Trina said.

"I'll pick you up around six on Friday. We can have dinner first."

"Okay, I'll be ready. Have a good night."

Getting back in the truck, he said, "For sure I will." Then he drove off.

Timmy, Tina's brother, said, "What you doing up in Kenneth's truck?"

"Boy, hush."

Timmy's twenty-eight years old, still home, with three baby mamas, works when he wants to. His parents keep him out of jail by paying his child support at least twice a year. Even Trina pays to keep him out of trouble and to keep her mom from being upset and stressed out.

"Trina," her brother yelled.

"What, Timmy?"

"I put a blunt on your dresser."

"Thanks. Now what do you want or need?"

"Nothin', sis, damn!"

Tim's friend Mel touched her butt.

She said, "Boy, stop…take your light bright ass home."

"Trina, I love you, girl."

"Good, nice to know," she stated.

Mel was a cool white dude. Her brother, Timmy, and Mel were close as two peas in a pod.

Timmy said, "Please don't put your hands on my sister's ass again, or I will kick your ass tonight."

"Tell your brother it's okay, Trina."

"Cool, Timmy, fuck him up!"

Trina loved to start shit when they got all fucked up together. Trina walked in the house.

"Mommy, I'm home."

"Well, it's about time. Where you been at?"

"Kenneth took me to have some dinner."

"Kenneth Brown?"

"Yes, ma'am," Trina said. "Mommy, he's so fine. I just wanted to take those sexy cherry lips and kiss them."

"Girl…you crazy."

"We going out Friday."

"So should I call the pastor and tell him Trina's in love again?"

"No, not yet, Mommy."

She went upstairs singing. Trina's phone rang, and she picked it up.

"Hello, Trina speaking."

"Hey, Trina, I seen your sneaky ass hugged up with Kenneth in the Soul Food restaurant."

"Mitch?"

"Yeah, it's me, and I'll be there in ten minutes." He hung up.

Trina jumped in the shower and put on some sweats.

Just then Timmy yells, "Trina, Mitch is downstairs."

"Tell him to come upstairs."

Trina was working on some new designs for a few dresses as Mitch came upstairs.

"Hey, Mitch, what's up?"

He kissed her on the neck. "What you working on?"

"A few dresses that Josh's going to make for me."

Josh was her fashion designer who made all her clothes she sketches out. He was the best out of every person she went to school with. So they're working together to make things happen.

Mitch said, "I brought you something."

"Mitch, I don't want any more gifts."

"Trina, open the damn bag," he said.

He bought Trina a new sketchbook, a case of pencils, and a gift card to a fabric store for whatever else she needed.

"Thank you, Mitch."

"No problem. I just wanted to drop the bag off to you. Come spend the night with me and just let me hold you—no strings attached."

"Now how the hell you goin' to explain to your wife you stayed out all night?"

"You let me worry about that."

So Trina got dressed.

She yelled, "Mommy, I'm out. Don't wait up," as she left with Mitch.

Mitch got a hotel room, and Trina walked in.

Then he said, "I'm going to take a shower, and then we can talk. Order some salad and fruit."

"Okay. No meat, right?"

"Right, babe."

When he came out in his towel with water dripping down his sexy body, she couldn't speak. He smirked, walking past her. He heard the knock on the door while getting a tip from his wallet. He opened the door taking the salad and fruit.

"Thanks."

Trina got undressed, putting on the robe hanging in the closet.

He stared her body up and down.

She sat down.

Mitch said, "Now you want to tell me what's going on between Kenneth and yourself?"

"No, because there's nothing to tell. My car broke down, he stopped and sat with me until my father got there, and we had dinner."

"Brownie point for Kenneth from your dad, huh? Aye, Trina, why did you tell your father I'm married?"

"I told him because my dad knows your father, okay." Trina told him, "You're married, and I wouldn't want any woman to sleep with my husband."

They got on the bed, and he held her that night—no sex. Trina lay there under the covers in her robe, thinking about Kenneth.

Around 5:00 a.m. in the morning, she woke Mitch up.

Looking into her eyes, he said, "I'm going to make this right one day, you'll see."

"I know you will, Mitch. Friends until then?" She kissed him.

They both got up, got dressed, and he took her home.

Trina began to start up the stairs, and her father yelled, "Trina, I want to see you." He was in the kitchen, waiting for her ass to come in the house. She went in.

"Morning, Daddy."

"Morning, Trina. Where've you been?"

"Out, Daddy."

"Let me tell you something right now. I didn't raise no tramps. So whatever you doing, *stop it*! Do I make myself clear?"

"Yes, sir. Daddy, it wasn't what you thought. I haven't did anything with Mitch. We talked, and I told him I could only be his friend. He's married, and I couldn't and wouldn't do that to his wife."

"*Trina*, got damn it, but you did! You stayed out with this woman's husband all night, even if you didn't sleep with him. Trina, you may be twenty-four, almost twenty-five, but I'll still put some leather to your skin. The next time you stay out all night and it's Mitchell Lee bringing you home in the morning, you tell him to back his truck up so you can get your shit out my house. You hear me, Trina?"

"Yes…"

"I didn't hear you, Catrina!"

"Yes, sir."

She went upstairs and cried. Her brother heard her crying, so he knocked.

"Go away," Trina said.

Timmy opened the door. "Lil' sis, I heard Dad. Did you really tell Mitch that, Trina?"

"Yes, I did, Timmy."

"Look, Trina, Dad's right on one point. You did stay out with Mitch even if you didn't have sex. He's married."

"Daddy's upset with me now."

"Trina, he can't stay mad at you for long."

She got ready for work and went down for breakfast. It was so quiet you could hear a pin drop. So Timmy tried to break the ice at the table.

"Hey, Trina, you still need me and Mel to come paint today?"

"Yeah! I also need you to find someone that can hang the ceiling fans for me."

"All right, I'll look around for some help."

Her father said, "I got to go, Lena. Call you later." He didn't say anything to Trina as he went out, but then he came back in after starting the truck. "Trina, your uncle and I will be at the shop around four thirty to start painting."

"Yes, sir."

Smiling at Timmy, he said, "Go get the paint she needs."

"Yes, sir."

Trina interrupted, "Love you, Daddy."

"Yes, and I love you too, but I meant what I said, Trina. Now I got to go."

Kenneth was at home talking to his parents. He said, "Mom, I met this nice girl. She fine, Mom. I mean, really fine."

"Kenneth, that's what you said about that damn girl Nikki!"

"Oh, Lawd, Mom, please be nice."

"Kenneth, I'm always nice to the tricks that come here to visit you."

His brother, Kent, bust out laughing.

"Hey, Mom, Kent playing hooky from school."

"Kenneth, you're always telling shit!"

Kenneth laughed, going up the stairs. "Kent, let's go," he said. "This is your last year, and I'll kick your ass if you fail college."

Kent was his twenty-one-year-old brother and in college to become a gynecologist and was almost finished. Kenneth helped his little brother out as much as he can and would do anything for him, but he's a little hard on him 'cause Kent's a mama's boy.

Trina called Kenneth as he was leaving for work. He smiled the whole way while talking to her. He asked Trina could he call her later. She said yes.

When her dad and uncle came, she was on the phone talking to Kenneth, giggling and smiling.

"Who she talking to, Timmy? Kenneth?"

Trina had been on the phone for an hour. She went out front talking on the phone, and it was cold-ass shit. She didn't even realize it was that cold while she was talking to him on the phone.

"Hey, Daddy, get you dumb daughter inside."

"Trina," he yelled.

"Yes, Daddy."

"Get your coat before you get sick."

"Yes, sir," she replied. " Kenneth, I'll see you tomorrow."

"Later, Trina," he said and hung up.

Trina said, "Daddy, he's so, so fine."

"Oh, Lawd. Trina, stock those boxes of shoes in the back."

"Billy, you ready for this romance to be built?" Willis asked.

"Yes, I see it happening," his brother answered.

"Well, at least he's not married or a daddy of six."

Trina said, "It's quitting time, fellas. I'm going to get my hair done and can't be late. Daddy, can you lock up 'cause Christine will leave without doing my hair. *Bye!*"

"*Got damn*, I'm telling you, Willis, the whole damn family on her mother's side is working off one cylinder…and that's a not a good thing."

Willis laughed and said, "Trina's a smart young lady when it comes to men."

"No, she's not clicking right, bro, I'm tryin' to tell you."

"Hey, Timmy and Mel, let's go."

"We done?"

"Yes, we done. For the last damn time, you, Mel, and Trina need to leave that bad weed alone. It's really fucking with the brain. Now let's go."

Trina arrived at the shop on time. Sittin' there, she decided on a style Marco had seen. Trina called her father and asked if he got her text.

"Yes."

"Do you like the cut, Daddy?"

"Trina, do you like it? Look, call me when your ass in trouble or stuck on the side of the road. Trina, don't call me about your damn hair. Call Lena for that bullshit. Love you and I'll see you later."

"Love you more, Daddy."

"Okay, let's do it," Marco said. "Christine, I got this."

Trina told Christine, "Yes, you never cut my hair this length."

The front door opened, and it was Mitchell's wife.

"Mitch's wife comes here?" Trina asked.

"Yes," Christine said and bust out laughing.

"Oh, Lawd, Marco, hurry up so I can get out of here."

"Fuck her, she needs to tame her man, then he won't stray," Lisa spoke to everyone.

Christine said, "Ann, your client's here."

Trina looked at Christine, smiling. Ann came out.

"Hey, Lisa, you can come in the back."

"Girl, she was in here one day talking to Ann saying, she knew the girl was light and had a nice shape and was short. But didn't know where she lived."

"Okay, Trina, let's wash and wrap your hair."

Trina had to sit under the dryer in the chair next to Lisa.

Trina told Marco, "You're a mess." She smiled.

"Now play nice, Trina."

Lisa didn't hear him though.

Mitchell walked in wearing his suit, still looking real good.

Christine said, "Hey, Mitch. Your women, I mean your wife's in back, under the dryer.

Marco said, "You shady, Christine," and he laughed.

Trina looked, and Mitch was so shocked to see them sitting next to each other. Trina spoke and kept texting Kenneth on her phone.

Mitch was paying for his wife's hair when Ken walked in with a sandwich and a drink for Trina.

Christine said, "Marco, no, let him take it to her. She is under the dryer."

Trina saw those bowlegs coming toward her and thought, *Shit!* "Kenneth, what you doing here?"

"I was going next door to get a haircut, and I saw the car outside. Here, eat this until you can leave. I know how long it takes for a woman to get it right in the hair salon."

"Thank you."

Mitch was boiling hot.

Then Marco came back and said, "Okay, boo, let get this hair sexy for your date tomorrow."

Ken said, "Yes, get it right." Ken gave Marco $200 and told him, "Give the nail tech $100 however she wants them."

"Kenneth, I can pay."

Mitch walked past and looked at Trina so pissed off.

Ken kissed her on the cheek and said, "Enjoy the sandwich, and I'll call you later."

"Okay, see you, and thanks, Kenneth."

Mitch finished talking to his wife, Lisa, and then began to walk out and looked at Trina again.

He said, "I'll see your ass later."

Marco bust out laughing 'cause boyfriend was in his feelings.

"Trina, did you give Mitch some ass?"

"No, but he did taste a little bit one night."

"Girl, that thing must be so kind of good. Maybe I should go straight."

"Bitch, finish my hair please, so I can go."

Marco got serious and focused on Trina's hair so she could get out on time and go home.

Lisa said, "I love your hair."

"Thank you. I got to go. This right here I can't do," she said, looking at Christine.

Trina stopped next door and said, "Kenneth, can I talk to you for a minute?"

"Sure."

The fellas was looking like, "What the fuck, and who the fuck is that?!"

Ken walked near the door and said, "What's up?"

"I can't let you pay for my hair and nails."

"Trina, I tell you what, you pay for dinner tomorrow."

"That's a deal."

Kenneth said, "I like when you call me Ken," as he winked at her. He touched her hair, smiling.

"Bye, Ken."

He opened the door for her, saying, "Lawdy, Lawdy," as she walked away. Ken walked back into the shop and sat in the chair.

Troy asked him if he and Trina were seeing each other.

"We going out tomorrow," Ken said.

"Man, she sexy."

Ken slid him five, and they laughed.

"That young sweet thing will be Mrs. Brown real soon. Watch and see."

Mitch walked in, and Ken started up.

"We meet again, Mr. Lee. How's the wife doing?"

"Kenneth, don't start your shit with me," Mitch said. "We don't roll like that. How's Nikki?" Mitch asked.

"I have no idea. Haven't seen her since I've been seeing Trina."

Those two went back in forth until Troy got his hair cut so he could leave.

"Hey, Mitch, I'll see you around."

"Fuck you, Kenneth, you bow-legged motherfucker."

"Mitch, what the fuck was that about?" Kelly, his barber, asked him.

"Man, you remember I told you I met this fine-ass phat-to-death chick?"

"Yes…wait, shorty that was just in here?"

"She was in here."

"Yes, talking to Kenneth. Her name's Trina."

"Yes, that's her. I fucked up and didn't tell her about Lisa, and she didn't want no more dealings with me."

"She fine, Mitch. No shit!"

Kenneth went home, took a long hot shower, had some dinner, and went upstairs. He was about to call Trina, when Nikki called.

"What's up, Nikki?"

"You want some company?"

"No, I'm straight. I need to get up early tomorrow."

"Kenneth, you fucking this bitch?"

"If I'm fucking, that's my business, not yours. Always remember that. And never address a lady as a bitch. We done talking, Nikki? I really need to go."

She hung the phone up.

He lay on his bed and turned the TV on. He called Trina.

Trina was in the tub when Kenneth called. She had just been cussed out by Mitch on the phone.

"Hello, Ken."

"What's up, short stuff?"

"Nothing much."

"What happened at the barbershop?"

"Nothing, why?"

"Just asking."

"Look, I didn't call you to talk about the shop. I called to see if you wanted to come snuggle with me, or maybe I can come cuddle with you?"

"You can come over here for a little bit."

"Your parents' home?

"No, Ken, they went to Virginia."

"I'll be there in couple minutes."

"Okay, Kenneth."

Trina got out the tub and put on her nightshirt and panties.

"Timmy, where you going at tonight?"

"Over my baby mama's house, why?"

"Ken's coming over."

"I'm going to need some hush money," he said.

Trina gave him $50 dollars. "Now get out my room."

Trina called her mother, and they was partying hard. "I just wanted to say good night."

Her mom, Lena, said, "We would be home about 4:00 p.m."

"Okay, see you and Daddy tomorrow. Love you both."

The doorbell rang. It was Ken. Trina went down and opened the door.

"Why you smiling, Ken."

"Can't I smile when I see you."

"Man, get in here."

Trina locked the door, and they both walked in and sat down in the living room.

"You want some wine, a beer?"

"I'll take a beer."

He watched Trina walk back toward him. "Why you so short, Trina?"

"Look! My mom and nana's short, okay?"

He laughed.

"So tomorrow, where you taking me for dinner?"

"Where you want to go? There's a new spot just opened up."

"Okay, sound good."

Ken and Trina talked, but Ken couldn't keep his hands off Trina.

"I thought we we're going to cuddle? I'll keep my clothes on. I promise."

Trina picked her glass of wine up and said, "Let's go."

"Lead the way."

Trina turned the light off, and they went upstairs.

Ken looked around in Trina's room and said, "Cute room."

"Thanks, sit down."

He put his coat on the back of the chair, and Trina got on her bed.

"Ken, you can turn the TV on."

"No, the jazz sounds pretty good."

"You like jazz?"

"Yes, my father plays jazz every day."

He lay on Trina's bed and asked for a kiss. She put a big wet kiss on those lips. Things started to get heated up in the bedroom.

Ken said, "Take your night clothes off so I can hold you for a few."

She stood up, and Ken told her how beautiful she was standing in the middle of the floor with just her panties on. Ken stood up and took his clothes off and said to Trina, "I won't bite."

They got in bed and talked as he held her tight. Trina could feel his dick getting harder and harder as she kissed him. He lay between Trina's legs and pulled her panties to the side, making her so wet. He took her panties off and began to finger her. Trina moaned as he made her feel good. Ken came out his briefs, and he said in her ear, "I want to make love to you."

"Yes," she said. "The condoms are in my draw."

He had already put his hard dick in her. He said, "Trina baby, this feel so damn good," while holding her tighter. "Baby, where's the rubber?

"In the draw," she answered.

He couldn't or just wouldn't stop to put get the rubber. He made Trina feel really special. She opened up wide, and he stroked dick all up in her.

Ken mumbled, "Oh, fuck," over and over.

Holding one of her legs in his arm, Trina was taking his hard strokes. Trina began to bite her bottom lip.

"Baby, I need to stop, like now."

Trina was hot and ready to explode.

Ken stopped and leaned over, getting a rubber. Trina started rubbing his legs as he was putting the condom on.

"Trina, you so beautiful."

She wasn't trying to hear him talk. She just wanted him to fuck her. Trina pulled him down on top of her and put his big sausage inside her. She said, "I want it from the back." She got on her knees, and he slapped that ass a few times as he gave her what she wanted.

"Girl, I'm about to break all this dick off inside you."

"Then give it to me."

Ken took his hand and slapped her ass so hard, setting her on fire.

"That's what you want, baby?"

"Yes," she replied.

He felt warmness from inside her tunnel.

Trina said, "Don't stop."

"No, baby, the rubber."

She put it on him so damn good, he couldn't even stop. "Uhhhh, shit! Baby, fuck. I'm coming, baby," he said as he grabbed her hips, riding that ass and releasing his cum inside her. He continued to work it until Trina finished getting hers.

After finishing all that good sex, Trina fell down on the bed, saying, "Shit!"

Ken looked down and asked Trina, "What just happened?"

"What?"

"The rubber?!"

"Shit," she said.

"I was telling you it bust. Can you get something like a plan B?"

"Yes, I'll get one tomorrow, Ken. I'm sorry, don't think I'm trying to trap you."

"Trina, chill. We both were in this together. Girl, that thangs good."

"Man, hush!"

Both of them got up, and Trina changed the sheets.

Ken said, "Can I take a shower?"

"Yes, the towels are in the closet."

"You coming?"

"You want me to?" she asked.

"Yes, please."

Getting in, he said, "Don't get your hair wet, Trina. We still have a date tomorrow."

"You still want to go out?"

"Yes. Why not, Trina? Look, whatever you heard about me, it may be true. But when I'm after something I want, I don't hit and quit, okay?"

They got all fresh, and Ken asked if she was hungry.

"A little, Ken."

"Well, get dressed and let's go grab a bite to eat. Look, I'm supposed to work tomorrow, but I would like to hang out with you. Take a drive or anything you want to do."

"Really, Ken?"

"Yes, now get dressed so we can eat."

"Do you want to stay over my house tonight so we can finish what we started?" He smiled.

Trina said, "You fresh, Ken."

She packed a bag and said, "Let me get my medicine."

"Please don't tell me you're crazy."

"No. I have irregular heartbeat and anxiety attacks when I get too overwhelmed, like fussing and fighting."

"Thanks for telling me. Baby, how you get all that ass in those jeans without oiling that ass."

"You have a lot of jokes, don't you, Ken?"

"No, baby, I'm just saying. And what size shoe you wear?"

"A size 5. Why?"

"Nothing."

She smiled. "What size shoe you wear, Ken?"

"Eleven and half. When it's hard, it's a twelve."

"Ken, you're sick."

"They keep telling me that. Can we please go now? Are you always this slow getting dressed?" he asked.

"Yes." She laughed. "Okay, I'm ready."

He took her bag, and they headed out the door.

Just then her ex pulled up.

"Trina, you know him?"

"Yes, give me one second."

Ken got in his truck.

It was Chris, who lived two doors down. She was in a relationship with him for two years. They broke up because she told him a lie and said she had an abortion, but she actually lost the baby while out partying one night and she fell down some stairs, but she didn't tell him the truth.

Trina walked over, saying, "What's up?"

"What, you avoiding me now?"

"No, Chris."

"We need to talk."

"I'll call you."

"You do that, Trina."

She walked away as he backed out.

Ken didn't asked her who he was. He asked, "You ready?"

"Yes, let's go."

"You okay?"

"I'm good."

Ken looked at the car dude was driving and the tags, then pulled off, tooting the horn at Chris. Then he smiled at Trina.

Trina said, "Oh, Lawd, I'm dealing with a nut."

"You got that right."

Ken stopped at his house to get his wallet and took Trina's bag inside. He came back out and asked, "What we eating?"

"It doesn't matter, Ken."

"How about pizza?"

"Okay."

"Do you want to stop and get that pill in the drug store?"

"Yes, please, I can take it in the morning."

He pulled in the parking lot. "Let's go, short stuff." Ken opened her door and took her by the hand.

He placed their order and said, "We'll be back in a few to be seated."

Walking down to the store together, he said, "Condoms?" smiling. "Trina, you not on the pill?"

"No, I haven't had sex in six months."

"What!"

"Long story."

Trina gave Ken the box and said, "Here you go."

He paid for their stuff, and they walked back up to the pizza shop.

When they were seated, Ken spotted a couple of ladies that hung out with Nikki. He spoke to them. Then he asked Trina, "You remember Nikki?"

"Yes, how can I forget her."

"Well, in a couple minutes my phone's going to ring because one of the ladies at the booth is going to call her and tell her I'm out with you."

"So, I don't care. You snooze you lose."

He laughed.

"Pizza for Brown?"

"Over here, my man."

"Ken, you sure you want to be sitting this close to me?"

"Yes, ma'am." He even gave her a kiss.

There it was, his phone went off, and he hit the earpiece.

"I been waiting for this call. What you want, Nikki?"

"Who the fuck you with?"

"Trina, why?"

"I hope you're having a great time. Lose my damn number, you sorry mother fucker."

"Okay, anything else, Miss Nikki? Bye, Nikki."

Trina yelled, "Hey, Nikki."

She said, "Hell no."

"Ho, ladies."

"You're a mess, Ken."

"I'm good. Look, I don't have a girlfriend. I have friends. They fall in love with me. I explain to them that I'm not trying to marry them or fall in love. But you, I'll go there. I'll hang up my single card to be with you."

"Really, Kenneth?"

"Yes, really. I'm ready to fall in love. I need to be tamed, whipped into shape. Can you handle that, Trina Jones?"

"Sure could."

"You keep throwing that thing on me like earlier, I might just go crazy over some, Trina."

She choked on her soda. "Ken, you're a nut."

Ken said, "Waiter, can I get a box and the bill, please."

"Yes, sir."

Ken held Trina, kissing on her neck.

"Ken, be nice now," she said.

Ken gave his card to the waiter and packed up the pizza.

"Let's go to the house and cuddle," he said, kissing her lips.

Trina stood up, putting on her coat.

Ken said. "Girl, you're so blessed," looking at her backside. "Shorty, get your bag."

"Don't worry, I am."

Ken waved, saying, "Good night, ladies." Then he said, "Now I know my brother's up, as always. My dad may be up, and my mom is asleep."

"Okay, how many women stay over your house?"

"None. Gwen not playing that shit. She doesn't like none of them."

Ken drove up to the front of the house. He walked around and opened the door for Trina and then grabbed the pizza. He opened the door with his key.

His brother, Kent, was lying on the sofa. He looked up and started smiling.

"What's up, bro?"

"Nothing much."

"Here's some pizza, greedy ass."

"Thanks. Hey there."

"Hello," Trina said. "You're a cutie."

"Oh hell, why you tell him that?"

"Hey, Daddy, Kenneth's home."

"Hey, son, I need to talk to you," he said as he came walking into the living room. "When you come home, park your truck in the damn driveway." Then he looked up and saw Trina standing beside his son. "Hello," he said, removing his glasses.

"Hi, Mr. Brown, nice to meet you."

"Likewise." He smiled. "*Damn*! You're pretty. Whose daughter you belongs to?"

"Dad! This Billy Jones's daughter."

"Lena and William Jones?"

"Yes, sir," Trina said.

"Tell your dad we need to get together soon when the weather get warm to go fishing."

"Yes, sir, I'll tell him."

"Trina, it's the first room on the right. You want a glass of wine?

"Sure."

"I'll be right up."

Trina went upstairs, and Ken stood talking to his father and brother.

His father said, "How you meet this fine young lady?"

"Daddy, she's fine, right?"

"Yes, indeed," Kent said. "Kenneth, she got a big butt."

He said, "Kent, eat the damn pizza."

"No, bro, it's a nice butt, nice and round."

"Dad, can you please let Mom know Trina's here. You know she be trippin'."

"I got you. Hey, don't do nothing I wouldn't do back in the day."

"Oh, Lawd. Good night." He started going upstairs.

Kent said, "The wine."

"Kent, good looking out." He got the bottle and two glasses and went up to his bedroom.

"Trina, you hot?"

"A little."

He turned the ceiling fan on and shut the window. Trina took her pills and got undressed, putting on a T-shirt. Ken poured the wine and got undressed. He did his sit-ups, then went in the bathroom. He came back out with a towel wrapped around his waist.

"Trina, you can take those panties off. My bed, my rules. So, Trina, what's up with the six months no sex?"

"I lost a child and me and the guy stop seeing each other," she said. "I told him one thing, and he found out I lost the child, and we broke up. It was dumb, and it's over now."

"You mean the dude with the white car tonight?"

"Yes. Chris. He's a good guy. Just was a little jealous at times. He lives near me."

"How long was you together?"

"Two years. Been knowing him for years though. He build bridges and is a very smart person."

"He's a mama's boy, and I'm a daddy's boy?"

"Yes."

"When I become a father, I want my son to be like my father and I. We are close. But I want him to also look out for his mom."

Ken and Trina snuggled in bed watching TV when Ken slid between Trina's legs, getting his night treat before going to sleep.

"Ken, what you doing?"

"You getting up taking the pill in the morning, right?"

"Yes."

"Okay then." He got his freak off and lay there holding her. "Baby, back that ass up on me."

"Good night, Ken."

He said, "I can't do this." He got up and got a blanket. "Living with you would be a bitch in the winter." Ken put some clothes on. "Trina, I sleep in the nude. Summer, I don't wear underwear."

"Me either."

Ken laughed.

"Good night, baby."

"Wow," Ken said, still laughing.

That morning, Ken's mom went up to Kenneth's room thinking he had overslept. She walked straight in the room and saw this pretty young lady in her son's arms, asleep.

"Kenneth, wake up."

He opened his eyes. "What's wrong, Mom?"

"It's seven forty-five, and I'm not going in the office today. Simms got it today."

"You cook breakfast?" he asked.

"Your father went to get breakfast this morning, and now I know why."

"Call my phone when the food comes."

"I sure will, so you and cutie pie can come down."

His mom left out his room.

Ken got up, shutting the fan off, and went in the bathroom. He came back out, climbing back in bed. Lying on his back, Trina found her way on his chest holding him. Ken looked down at her sleeping and kissed her forehead.

They slept until Ken's phone rang at 9:00 a.m. It was his mom.

"Hello, Kenneth, y'all come down and eat. Okay?"

"Baby, wake up."

Mom said, "Come eat."

"Okay."

Trina sat up, looking crazy. She said, "I need some sweats or shorts."

He went in his closet and got her some sweatpants. She went in the bathroom, took her pills, brushed her teeth, and washed her face. Trina combed her hair, and she put on his slippers.

"Ken, where's my bag at?"

He said, "Here."

She took the pill and said, "Okay, let's go eat."

Ken went downstairs, putting on his T-shirt.

"Good morning."

His parents said, "Good morning."

Trina walked in behind Kenneth.

"Short stuff, have a seat."

"Good morning," his mom said. "I'm Gwen, Ken's mom. Nice to meet you."

"I'm Trina Jones."

"Yes, I know your mom, Lena. We go to the same church every Sunday, but I haven't seen you in church in a while."

"No, ma'am, I been working to get my store opened, but it's about ready."

"Mom, where's the bacon at?"

"Kenneth, seat down, please."

He fixed Trina's plate.

"Ken, that's too much."

"You need to eat. Holding you around the waist is like holding a stick."

"She has a cute figure, Kenneth."

"Yes, I know Trina got it going on."

Miss Gwen said, "Think of her body like a cola bottle. Shit, I wish I looked like that."

Ken's dad smiled. "Gwen, you look good to me."

"Well, thanks, Kenneth Sr. Your nails are beautiful, Trina."

"Thank you. So are yours, Miss Gwen." Then Trina said to Ken, "Ken, that's apple butter. You want some?"

"Yes. No almonds, Mom. Trina can't have any kind of nuts."

"So that means I'm going to see more of this young lady?"

"I'm hoping so," Ken said, looking at Trina. "Juice, Trina?"

"Yes, please."

"It's calling for some snow today."

"Short stuff, let's go get ready before it snows."

"Where we going?"

"For a ride in the country."

Trina went up and took a shower while Ken was at the door with Nikki's crazy ass, getting his bag of clothes that was left at her house.

"Thanks. Now take your dumb ass home, Nikki."

She went to spit at Ken, and he grabbed her by the neck, pushing her head into the front door. "Bitch, you will die today! Now take your ass home before I stick these eleven-and-a-half in your ass, Nikki. You heard me, right?"

"Yes. Now let me go, please."

"Don't bring your ass around here anymore. And if I hear you said one thing to Trina, I will fuck you up in a way you won't see coming. Now take your ass home!"

Ken got his bag, took his clothes, and put them in the washer. Then he went upstairs.

Trina said, "You okay?"

"Yes, why wouldn't I be?" He kissed Trina and went to take a shower.

Trina sat down and called her mom.

"Good morning, Mother."

"Hey, daughter."

"I called since I'm over Kenneth's and ready to go on a country ride before it snows out there. Mommy, I know you don't care if we have company. I just wanted to let you know first. So tonight Ken may stay over, but I'm not sure."

"Okay. Look, you're going on twenty-five, ready to get your own shit soon, I hope. And as long as you show respect, you bring who you want to."

"We might. If I stay out, I'll call you later."

Ken asked, "Baby, do you want to stay at your house tonight or here?"

"Neither," she smiled. "Let's get a room, chill, and hope to get snowed in together. So go grab something warm, a heavy coat, and let's hit the road."

They went downstairs and told everyone, "See you tomorrow."

"Where y'all going?"

"Me and Trina going to elope. Bye, Mother."

"Kenneth, don't play with me," Miss Gwen said.

Trina went to her house and grabbed a couple outfits and even a sweater dress to wear.

"You got everything you need?"

"Yes."

Ken pulled off, and they ended up in North Carolina.

"Let's get a hotel room and watch the snowfall this weekend."

It was a big beautiful hotel, just built.

"Can we get a suite for two days? Wait, make it until Sunday."

"Great choice. Snows about to hit us."

Trina walked away.

"Sir, do you have a justice of the peace nearby?" Ken asked.

"My brother's one, and he's across from the hotel."

"If he can fit me in tomorrow around noon, I'll make it worth it, for both of you."

Ken wrote all the information down for him and Trina.

"The license will need to be mailed to you."

"That's fine. He'll file that Monday.

"I'm on it."

"I'll call you in a few, Mr. Brown."

"Ken, what you doing?" Trina asked.

"Oh, nothing."

"Let's go. I want to take you to meet my grandparents."

The suite was huge.

"We are staying here until Sunday."

"I only brought two outfits and a sweater dress."

"I'll get you whatever you need."

"How about we go visit my nana another time?"

"No, let's go now."

The front desk called Ken, saying, "He could do the wedding ceremony today at 5:00 p.m., and it could be filed by 5:30 p.m."

"So today?"

"Yes, Sir."

"Okay, thanks."

So Ken and Trina went riding and decided to just hang out and go see Nana on Saturday. They hit the bar and got toasted, I mean, ducking wasted.

"Catrina, let's get married right now."

"What?"

"Marry me, baby. If it's not for you, we'll undo this mistake, but I don't think this will be a mistake. We can do it the right way for the family, or we can keep it a secret until Christmas."

"What you say, Ken? I don't know about this."

"Say yes." He kissed her. "Trina, I have fallen for you. I'm in deep, and I know you're too. I feel it when you touch, kiss, and make love with me. What do you say?"

"Our parent are going to kill us."

"No, they won't."

"Okay, this may be the craziest thing I ever did in my life."

He got out and walked around, and they both sprayed their mouths from drinking cognac.

"Mr. Brown, I thought you changed your mind."

"No, not at all," Ken said as he looked at Trina.

And they got married.

Mr. and Mrs. Brown both signed on the dotted line. Ken paid the guy very well.

Ken said, "You can send everything to my office." He gave the clerk his address." He told Trina, "Look, it's okay. Stop stressing."

The snow came falling down as Ken and Trina ordered a big dinner up to the suite.

"To us, baby."

"Now what, Ken?"

"Nothing, we go home and do as we always do until Christmas. I will ask you to marry me, and go from there."

They enjoyed that whole weekend away, snowed in together. Now it was time to go home.

Ken dropped Trina off, going in to say hello to her parents. He said, "Call me later. Get some rest."

"I will. Hey, I love you."

"Ditto," he said, smiling.

"Mr. Billy," Kenneth said. "Get with my Dad because he's planning a fishing trip soon. Tell him to text me the information. I'm down for whenever.

"Yes, Sir. Later, Love. So how was your little getaway with Kenneth?"

"It was really nice," Trina said. "What's for dinner?"

"Beef and rice," Miss Lena said.

"Okay, I'm going to lay down for a hour." Trina went up to her room and logged on the Internet. Ken had just posted a picture of them, which said, "She got me on lock with the gold seal." Trina posted, "Never in my wildest dreams would I be with this man" with a picture of them in the hot tub drinking champagne.

Their pages were blowing up.

Next, Ken posted, "Lay down, baby, been a long drive back home."

She replied, "Can't sleep. Come on over."

"I'll call you in a few."

Mitch called Trina.

"Hey, Mitch, what's up?"

"You sneaky ass."

"What, Mitch?" She laughed.

"Trina! Stop playing, I'm being serious."

"I know you are. Listen, you have another life with Lisa. I would be yours, but you're married, and I can't do that to her."

"But why Kenneth?"

"Hey, I could have said the same about you."

"I want you and Ken to be nice to each other, Mitch."

"I'll try, Trina."

"If I tell you something, will you keep it to yourself?"

"I don't know."

"Never mind, Mitch."

"No, I'm only joking because I care about you."

"We went to North Carolina, and we got married."

"What!"

"Mitch, please don't say anything. My parents, they don't even know."

"Awww, Trina!" He laughed. "Hey, well at least Mr. Jones won't be looking at me crazy now."

"Mitch, you can't say anything."

"I won't. You did what me and Lisa did on Faith."

"I guess so."

"Trina, do you care about him?"

"Yes, I been crazy about him since college."

"You love him?"

"I have fallen deeply in love, and he makes me do crazy, silly things. I get nervous around him too."

"Okay, I'm happy for you, not for him. He all up in my pie though."

"Bye, Mitch."

"Later, Brown." He laughed.

Trina walked downstairs and ate some dinner.

"You couldn't sleep?"

"No, ma'am."

Timmy walked in and said, "Sis, what's up?"

"Nothing much. Chris said stop down. He needs to talk to you."

"About what?!"

"Look, I don't know and don't shoot the messenger."

Trina got up grabbed her coat and went down to see Chris. She knocked on the door, and he opened it, telling her to come in.

"Where your man at?"

"Chris, what do you want?

"Why the fuck you keep avoiding me for?"

"I'm not doing this with you tonight. Matter-of-fact, I'm not doing this at all. Now move."

He stood in front the door.

"Move, Chris."

"That's right, get mad, cry and run home like you always do, you spoiled brat!"

"Cry?"

"Trina, if you were a man, I would kick your ass. Right here, right now."

"I want you to feel what I feel. You could have told me, Trina."

"Told you what?"

"You was having my baby."

"Here we go again. How many times are you going to keep saying the same thing over and over? I'm sorry I didn't tell you I was pregnant. I'm sorry I told you I got rid of the baby. We had a big falling out, and you was talking to Val again, so I did what I thought was best at the time."

"You don't know real love when it's standing in your face, do you? *Do you*!" he yelled in her face. "Trina, you're a heartless bitch!"

She slapped him in the face and walked out.

Trina went to her house and said, "I'm out."

"What, you and Chris had it out again?"

"I don't want to talk about it. I'm going over the Browns." She kissed her parents good night.

Her father asked, "Do you need to go on and move in with the Browns?"

"No, I'm just ready to get my own place. Maybe with Mr. Ken Brown. Bye!"

Trina's father said, "He couldn't handle living with your crazy ass."

Trina called Ken.

"You on your way, little mama?"

"Yes."

"Okay." He hung up.

In his pj's and slippers, he went down to let Trina in the house. It was Trina's first time seeing him in his glasses.

"Daddy, watch how slow Trina takes to get out the car."

"What she doing?" Mr. Brown asked.

"I don't know, but I'd be drained watching her."

His father laughed.

"Baby, will you come on."

"I'm coming. I dropped my phone case between the seat, and I can't get it.

"Trina, I'll give you mine."

"Ken, go find the damn case."

He walked outside and pulled the seat back. "Here, love."

She said, "Thank you," giving him a kiss.

Ken said, "You're going to be a pain-in-my-ass kind of wife, I see."

"No, I just wanted my case, so I won't break this phone."

"All right, baby, go in the house."

"Hi, Mr. Kenneth," she said, giving him a hug. "Where's your mom?"

"Gone to visit her sister and won't be back until Friday."

"Thank God."

"Daddy, you're wrong."

"Fuck if I'm wrong. Look, dealing with court all day, then come home to Gwen asking me third-degree questions, I need a break."

"I got a meeting in the morning."

"I guess we both do."

"Good night."

Trina walked in front of Ken, going upstairs. "I'm about to tear that ass up," he said.

"Kent, how you doing?"

"I'm good, and you?"

"Can't complain," Trina replied.

"Kent, hurry up off my computer.

"Let me use your laptop."

"You have thirty minutes, Kent."

Trina said, "Honey, don't get mad, but Chris wanted to speak to me."

"Okay and what happened?"

"He called me a heartless bitch."

"Oh, really."

"He's still going in about the baby and I should have told him."

"Okay, you apologized, right?

"Yes."

"And you explained why you didn't tell him?"

"Yes."

"Okay, let it go. Stop stressing about Chris. I'm working on something for us."

"What?"

"If I tell you, it wouldn't be a surprise."

Kent came back in the room and said, "Here's your laptop."

Ken told Kent to fly away like a bird. Trina told Kenneth stop being mean to him.

"Bro, lock my door on your way out."

Ken got naked and so did Trina. Ken told her, "Just worry about me being nice to you right now." He pulled the condoms out, looked at them, and tossed them on the floor.

"Ken, what you doing?"

"What you mean, girl? You better stop acting crazy and give me the cookies."

She laughed.

"Look, we're married, so all that stuff you talking, I'm not trying to hear it. Let's make a baby."

"Are you serious?"

"Yes," he said, kissing on her neck. "Mrs. Brown, come to daddy." He clapped his hands, turning the lights off.

Getting busy, Kent went down and said, "Dad! Do you hear those two upstairs?"

"Kent, I'm trying not to hear my son having sex over my head."

"If Mom was home, it would be on."

"Well, she's not, Kent. Now go to bed!"

"How can I go to sleep listening to Kenneth bang his girl?"

It got quiet. Ken was moving around, and a couple minutes later the water came on. Ken and Trina was in the shower together for round two. Ken moaned so loud that Trina held his mouth as he got his nut.

"Ken, put me down 'cause you are loud."

"Look, it was good, okay? Your hair, baby."

Trina showered and got out and wrapped her hair while Ken slipped his pj's on, then went down to get some ice cream.

"Bro, what's up?"

"You and Trina making all that noise."

"Sorry, my bad."

"Little loud," his father said. "I'm more sure her parent heard her at their house."

"What! I'll be a little more quiet next time." He fixed his ice cream and sat down.

"Trina didn't want any ice cream?"

"No, she asleep by now." Ken was smiling. "Kent, don't you have school in the morning?"

"Sure do."

"Well, good night then. Remember who invested their money in your education."

"I'm going to pay you back every dime when I become a doctor."

"Okay, well, bro, until then, good night."

Kent went back up to bed.

"Hey, Dad, I want you to go with me tomorrow evening to look at this house around the corner."

"You moving?"

"Yes, if I tell you something, you gotta promise you won't tell mom or Kent. Not even Nana."

"What, Trina pregnant?"

"No, I'm working on that." He smiled. "No, we went to North Carolina, and we got married."

"Stop playin' with me, Kenneth."

"I'm not. At Christmas, I'm going to ask her in front of everyone, and then we'll go to the courthouse, or you can even marry us, just for show. Daddy, it may sound crazy, but I been trying to get with Trina since college. And, Dad, I really love her."

"Ken, you sure about that? I mean, all the females you be seeing."

"I'm done with all that."

"I'll keep quiet. Congrats, son. So now what?"

"We just do this back in forth for now until I get this house. I hope in a few weeks or so.

"I'll go with you after work."

"I have an appointment at four thirty."

"Okay, I'll meet you here."

Ken went up to bed and woke Trina up. "Hey, you take your pills?" he asked.

"Yes, I did."

He lay down and went to sleep.

When Ken met with his dad, they went and looked at the house near his parents and in walking distance. He loved it, and the house was move-in ready. Ken decided to rent it since he wanted to move out of state in a couple years. He signed the lease and wrote the check. He was handed the keys. Ken wasn't playing. He took off work to move in the next day and went and paid $1,000 dollars extra to have the house furniture delivered. He called Trina and told her to come to the address. It took her about twenty minutes to get there. He opened the door and was smiling.

"What's up, husband?"

He laughed, saying, "Welcome home."

"What you talking about?"

"This ours until we build our dream house. It's a rental, baby, so don't go crazy."

"I love it." Looking out back, she saw a pool. "Ken, when can we move?"

"Well, my clothes are here and your clothes are being packed right now. Your mom and the movers are doing it. Stop playing and come look."

"What, baby?"

He took her up to the master bedroom and the huge king-size bed. "We are breaking this in tonight."

Trina was so happy that she and Ken was about to start a life together. She couldn't wait to start a family with him. Kenneth was trying hard to make it happen.

That night Trina and Ken worked so hard in their new place getting unpacked, but they did it. They just sat there looking around at the place they would call home together.

Trina said, "I'm so glad I broke down on the side of the road. 'Cause, Ken, if I hadn't, you and me wouldn't be in this place right now."

"I was trying to get with you, Trina, so it would have been a matter of time for us to be together."

"Oh, really?"

"Yes, I was asking around town about you, and people just said, 'She's dealing with some brown-skin dude.'"

Trina laughed. "Ken, stop lying."

"No. I was trying to get with you for a while and you just wouldn't give me the time of day."

"Well, I'm here now. Let's go to bed and work on our baby," she told Ken.

"Come on. I'm ready." He picked Trina up and carried her upstairs into the bedroom.

That night was a beautiful night.

The next morning, they got up and got ready for work and decided to go out to have breakfast.

While in the diner, Chris walked in. He walked over and said, "Hey, Trina, you have some things at my place."

"Can you just throw them in the trash?"

Ken said, "My man, don't you see us having breakfast?"

Chris stepped to Kenneth.

Ken stood up and said, "Now what? Take a good look around." He smiled.

Every worker here has my back and strapped.

"Now, you sure you want to come at me while I'm having breakfast?"

"Ken, please just sit down," Trina told him, getting upset. "Chris, please just toss the clothes or take them to my house."

"Yeah, I'll see you later, Trina."

"Dude, you making heavy remarks to my lady."

"Your lady...motherfucker, if I want that ass, I can get it."

"Oh, really. You may have got it in the past, but that was before I came along. Just remember these four words—Kenneth Brown I do."

Chris said, "Whatever." He grabbed his bag of food and left.

"I want to know if he come at you again. Trina, you heard me?"

Yes, Kenneth. So I will be busy after work. I'm going to play ball with Cleo."

"That's what you gonna do tonight?"

"I'll get a movie and popcorn for later."

"Is that what you want to do tonight, Trina, or do you want to go out?"

"We can for a little bit." She smiled at him.

"Mrs. Brown, don't get no ideas. We not staying out long."

"Yes, daddy."

"Okay, you think Shelly and her friend would like to go?"

"Yes!"

Trina asked her.

"I will, Kenneth. New Year's we going to New York, and we'll leave that Thursday since I need to handle some business."

"Okay. Sounds good."

"So, see, she wants to go. I will call everyone today."

Getting in the truck, Cleo looked at Ken pulled up saying, "Clothes finish about now?"

"I hope so," Ken said. Trina rolling her eyes at the both of them.

"Trina, are we packed for our trip?" Trying to change the subject.

"No, when we get home, I'll start packing."

Cleo stopped in the Laundromat and got back in the car with a backpack.

Trina said, "Wait one damn minute, why are we at the laundromat?"

Cleo yelled, "Trina, chill and stop buggin'."

He followed to Ken's truck, they went straight to Cleo's brother's shop where they looked over Ken's truck from top to bottom to see if it was bugged. And damn if it wasn't.

Ken said, "Motherfuckers."

Cleo tossed it in the river near the shop. "So now what?"

"Do exactly what was planned and then chill, bro."

"Yes, I agree. It's getting real hot. I see, Ken.

"I need to roll with my brother. I'll pick up that package up in the morning so you can make this move."

"Bro, stay safe."

"It's all love, but lil' mama is pissed right now, so I need to tell her what's really up."

Kenneth got in the truck and nothing was said until they got home. His lawyers were sitting outside waiting for them.

"Trina, wait get in the car."

"Now what, Kenneth?"

"Look Trina, just get in the car, please."

Standing outside the car, he opened the door and they both got in the car with the lawyers who explained everything to them.

Trina said, "Wait! I'm the owner of all Ken's businesses?"

"Yes, Trina, since he changed it a couple weeks ago. So please sign on this line."

Trina said, "Okay," smiling.

Ken told her, "Don't get no ideas, a'ight? This right here's for show, Trina."

"All money has been transferred into a new account already."

"Wait, I haven't signed for any accounts yet."

"Trina, here is your checkbooks and bank cards."

"I'll take one of those cards, thank you." He took it out her hand. "And all your paperwork, Trina."

"So Kenneth can't go and withdraw out this account?" she asked.

"No, only you."

"But how did you do this?"

"Money talks and bullshit walks. Kenneth's in good hands with you."

"Yes, he is."

"Okay, we're done, Kenneth."

"Thank you."

"See you both in a few weeks. And, Kenneth, please stay out of trouble."

"I'll try, Steven."

Trina went in the house and sat down to read all the paperwork. She wasn't no dummy when it came to business. Trina had handled all her grandfather's business in Atlanta for him.

That was her major in college, and she very great at it. Hell, she tutored the whole football team one semester in math and business.

Ken walked in the house, and Trina asked, "So we have over a billion dollars in the bank?"

"I have that amount in the bank. We were not married yet."

"Boy, hush!" Trina.

"What's for dinner?"

"Order something," she said, looking at all his bank statements. She yelled, "You dirty, nasty dog!"

"What now, Trina?"

"What bitch you took to the hotel the day you was on the side of the road with me."

"Baby, that's old shit, so let's not go there. Did I ask you who you were doing after I dropped you off?"

"And I'll never tell." She laughed.

"Trina, let's go out and eat down at the sub shop."

"Let's go so I can get back and pack."

"I'll go start the truck."

Trina put her shoes on. Her phone rang, and it was Mitch.

"Hey, Mitch, what's up?"

"I need your help."

"Okay, talk to me."

"I need you to sing with me on Thursday night at 8:00 p.m."

"You kiddin, right?"

"No, I'm dead serious."

"Thursday…okay. Ken's card parties that night. Okay, you owe me, Mitch."

"Where?

"At Ken's club."

"Are you got damn crazy."

"Trina, please."

"Okay, okay, don't you say nothing to nobody. I need to find a way to do this without him knowing."

"Uh, Trina, it's his club."

Ken blew the horn.

"Look, I got to go."

"Come to the studio Wednesday."

"Yeah okay." She walked outside and got inside the truck.

"I was talking to Mitch."

Ken was backing out and slammed on his brakes. "Please repeat what you just said."

"You heard me, Ken. Come on, man, let's go. I'm getting hungry and so is your child."

"Don't do that, Trina. Don't use my child to save your big ass. What did Mitch want with you?"

"Just to say hello."

"Yeah, okay. Don't let Mitch get a beatdown."

"He's my friend."

"All right, friend." Ken started driving. He said, "Trina, there's Chris."

"So what, Kenneth. Just drive to the subshop."

"There's Shelly too." Ken blew at her and pulled in a parking space.

Trina jumped out and went over, talking to Shelly and her boyfriend who was home for a week.

Shelly was doing the long-distance relationship. It worked for her. Trina smiled, seeing her ex in the back seat. "Congrats on the little one. Thanks, we just found out."

Ken waved and asked Trina, "What you want?"

"Whatever you order."

He went inside.

Terry told Trina that he just want to break his damn legs. "Maybe he'll walk straight, bow-legged bastard."

"Now why you need be calling names, Terry?"

"Trina, come see me later."

"NOT!"

Shelly bust out laughing. "You know Trina and Kenneth live together."

Trina said, "Bye, boy." Trina walked into the store, and Ken was on the phone talking to some dude in New York.

"I'll be there around noon tomorrow in my hotel lobby." Ken then told him, "Until then," and hang up.

"Honey, what you order?"

"Wings and a cheese steak. I forgot your fries." Ken yelled, "Mama Kim, fries also. And I want hot fries."

She was fussing at Ken in Chinese.

"Mrs. Kim, I understand you very well. Keep talking shit. So, baby, I have a meeting when I get there. And after that, we go shopping. Make sure you have warm clothes if we are walking around to shop."

"Shelly, Greg, and Christine still coming to New York?"

"Yes, I can't wait."

"Kenneth's orders up," Miss Kim yelled.

"See, she showing off today, Trina. I think she mad that you're in here."

"Kenneth, she can have you." Trina sat there, getting her eat on.

Chris walked in with his friend, Val. He spoke, and Trina spoke back.

Ken said, "Eat, baby. You alright, don't let small things worry you." He looked at Val and said, "Don't act cute."

"Hey, Kenneth, what's been up?"

"Nothing much."

"I see," he said, looking at Chris.

"Kenneth, you're a mess."

"Trina, I was trying to get her number awhile back."

And ole girl said, "Hell to the no…I don't do light men."

Trina said, "Can we please go, Ken. I don't want you showing your other side."

"And if we leaving, we're going home. What do you have planned?"

Trina smiled, leaned over, kissed him on the lips, and said, "You and me in the bedroom."

"All right, lil' mama, keep talking to me."

She bust that bubble and told him, "You helping me pack for New York. Now let's go."

"That's some cold shit, Trina." Kenneth helped her into her coat and kissed her on the lips. "Let's go. Miss Kim, we need a bag please. No egg rolls, Miss Kim."

She said, "Go home, Kenneth."

"Yes, ma'am, have a great night."

Kenneth looked at Chris and rolled his eyes like a female.

Chris just laughed, telling him he was so funny as Ken turned around.

Trina said, "Ken, let's go, please."

"But baby."

At home the couple packed for their little trip and went to bed. Trina had Chris on her mind that night and end up fucking Ken to death. After a great night of sex, they both went to sleep exhausted.

Ken was awakened by a security call from his building, so he had to go there. He slipped out of bed and went to his office.

While Ken was gone, Chris tapped on the window of their home.

It scared Trina. She looked out and saw Chris. "Man, are you crazy?"

"No, we need to talk."

"Chris, you've been drinking. Go home. I will talk to you when I get back home. I'm not playing, okay. Please go, Chris."

Trina got back into bed and just lay there. Ken came back about an hour later.

"Baby, get up. We need to go in a few."

"I'm up, Kenneth."

They showered together and got dressed so they could leave on time.

"Baby, we'll stop on the road for something to eat."

"That's fine," Trina said, taking her meds as they left the house.

Ken put some relaxing slow jams on; and Trina sat, undoing her pants, saying, "I feel much better."

Ken told Trina, "That phat ass getting too big."

"You like?"

"Yes, indeed, I do."

Ken stopped by Cleo's to pick up the book bag.

"Man, please be careful."

"I will, and I'll call you when it's done."

"Much love, but I need to go."

Kenneth stopped to get breakfast, and then they hit the road.

Trina slept almost the whole way there.

Kenneth wasn't playing, getting there on time, pulling into the hotel and getting checked in. He left, leaving Trina for an hour, to take care of business downstairs in the hotel.

They talked, had a drink, switched bags, and went their own way.

Going up on the elevator, a female joined Kenneth and he gave her the bag. She got off and hit the steps. He stayed on the elevator, going up to get Trina. They headed out to go shopping together. Kenneth placed a call to Cleo.

"Hey, we here and heading out now. It's a beautiful day."

That was the signal. It was done.

"Okay, I'll see you Saturday, bro. Can't wait."

"Later," Ken said and ended the call.

When Ken told Chris he could do everything for Trina, keeping her happy in designer clothes, shoes, and handbags, dude wasn't lying. He dressed her from head to toe.

Trina wanted to eat and was tired of shopping on an empty stomach.

Ken had to find a spot that sold rice. So the first Chinese spot they saw was where they ate.

Trina was in heaven eating with chopsticks.

"Trina, don't think you feeding our child no rice the whole pregnancy. He needs healthy food."

"I know, Ken. Just let me enjoy my food, please."

Later, he decided to get a tattoo with Trina's name on his chest in big bold letters. Trina sat down and waited until he was done, then they headed back to the hotel.

They both were beat and called it an early night in bed.

Chillin' the next evening, Ken and Trina went over his buddy Mark's house and had a good time. Trina was kicking it with Kenneth's homeboy and his girl, Zena. She didn't mind stepping out with the boys every now and again.

"Ken, come here please."

"What's up?"

"We going in the back."

Kenneth said, "Go ahead."

His buddy said, "Kenneth, let's have a drink and watch the flick." He smiled. "Then we can go join them."

"Mark, you must was reading my mind. Just like old times. Look, until I get married, I'm still the man. I'll let her dip until then. I'm telling your ass now. Mark, don't be falling in love with the pussy. Your first and last dip into my cookies, got it?"

"Man, I got this."

They got their drink on and watched Trina and Zena get it on with each other.

"Man, Trina's phat as hell."

"Zena's not too bad herself."

They went back and joined the ladies. They got undressed, and Ken kissed Trina. Mark tossed Ken a rubber. Mark put one on and slid in the bed, lying next to Trina. Ken and Zena hit the floor.

Trina said, "Ken."

Mark started kissing on Trina's neck, lying on top of her. He was big down below. He opened her legs and licked, getting her nice and wet. Trina could hear Zena down below enjoying Kenneth and so was Kenneth. Mark put his large dick in Trina and held her ass. Trina held on to the sheets as he fucked her like she was his bitch.

"This pussy's real good. Yes, open up for me. Take it all. You like it?"

"Yes." She got into the groove real fast.

"I want to *cum inside*," he said in her ear.

"No." And she started to push him off her.

"Okay, chill," he said as he continued to fuck Trina until he nutted.

"Yo, Kenneth, you had enough down there?"

He got up to let Zena hit the shower.

Ken pulled the rubber off and told Zena, "Toss that for me." Then he said, "Trina, everything okay, baby?"

"No, Kenneth, it's not."

He told Trina, "Come here," and kissed her in the mouth, smelling like Zena's pussy. Ken began to have sex with Trina, and she told him to stop.

"I'm ready to leave."

"Baby, we will in a few," Ken said, "after I get some. So turn over."

"When we get to the hotel," she replied.

"So you don't love me…it's your way or nothing? Fine, maybe this was a mistake, Trina."

"What? This?"

"No, us, baby. You knew what kind of person I was when you met me."

"Ken, let's just finish so we can go."

"I want it all."

"What, Kenneth!"

"You, me, and Mark. Hey, Mark, come in here."

"What's up, bro?"

"Close the door."

"Hey, Zena, go downstairs after you shower."

"Okay, just hurry up."

"Girl, shut the fuck up, and just do as I say."

Ken kissed Trina while Mark dropped his towel and went down on her.

Ken said, "Baby, give me some head."

She looked at him. She felt so cheap.

He rubbed his hard dick in her face and around her lips until she began to suck his dick while Mark began to fuck Trina.

"Hey, gently, Mark."

"I got this, bro," he said. "This pussy's the shit dude, if I must say so." He held her legs up and bust a nutt inside her again, making all types of noises and shit.

Trina wanted to cry, but she didn't. What really hurt was Ken went right after Mark and fucked her also, getting his nutt. After he was done, he said, "Get dressed so we can go."

Trina slipped her clothes on and had sperm running out into her panties. She felt so dirty.

Mark and Zena had the time of their lives.

"Bro, see you next week. You can stay with us."

"Cool. See you, Trina had a great time."

Zena said, "Trina, call me."

"I will, Zena."

After Trina got in the truck, Ken said, "What's wrong?"

"Ken, just leave me alone. I'm pregnant, and you let your friend cum inside me. You're sick, Kenneth."

"If you want to go to the doctors when we go home, we can."

"No, I'll take a test on my own. I don't need my doctor looking at me crazy," Trina said. "Stop at the store so I can get something. I feel so dirty right now."

He stopped, and she went in the store and got everything she could possibly get to clean herself. Trina got back to the hotel and took a hot bath and cleaned herself out.

She said, "You get none the rest of our stay here."

Trina went to bed mad.

Everyone arrived in New York together. Mrs. Brown wasn't feeling Kenneth at the moment, but he tried to put on a front around everyone that was there for the weekend. Behind closed doors, his ass was sleeping on the sofa.

That morning Trina got up, got dressed, and asked the girls if they want to go with her while she got her haircut.

"Trina, no…we'll stay here."

"I got to go."

"Trina, wait. We're going. What the hell is wrong with you?"

"*Life*, that's what's wrong."

"Baby, where you going? We're leaving in a couple hours," asked Kenneth.

"I know that. I'm going to get my haircut."

"What hair, Catrina? Okay, you come back in here with your hair all chopped off, and there's going to be a problem."

"Kenneth, kiss my ass," she said. Then ole girl just grabbed her purse and walked out.

"Greg, did she just tell me to kiss her ass?"

"Yes, indeed. What did you do to her, Ken?"

"Long story. If Trina wasn't pregnant, I would go drag her ass back in here and beat the living hell out of her. But I'll leave her alone for now."

Trina got in the truck. She looked at Shelly and Christine and told them about the little get-together. They already knew how Trina got down with females since college.

Trina said, "He let his buddy fuck me while he watched."

"Wait, hold up. You kidding, right?"

"No, Christine."

"And now y'all gettin' married on Friday?"

"Trina, you marrying Ken?"

"Yes, I'm going to marry Ken. I have too much invested in that ass. So I'll be his trophy wife, and only thing he's not old, but he can be that daddy he want to be."

"Trina, you stupid."

"No, I'm being very smart."

"Look, ladies, pussy don't come cheap. My mother said, 'It cost to be the boss.' You want me to spread open, it's going to cost, so all that you doing, just remember who holds the accounts."

Girlfriend went and said, "Cut my hair in the sexiest style you can do."

"Yes, ma'am."

And the guy put it down and made her look like a different person. *Sexy* wasn't the word.

Christine said, "That's nice. I love that cut. Kenneth's going to flip."

"Fuck Ken!" Trina looked in the mirror at her hair and loved it. She gave him a big tip. "Okay, ladies, let's go."

"I'm glad we not riding with you home."

Getting back to the hotel, Ken was checking Trina out, and if eyes could kill, Trina would be dead.

"Catrina, you a big girl now, I see."

"Boy, bye."

She got on the elevator.

"Shelly, why you didn't talk her out of getting that done?"

"Trina's her own woman, and that's her head."

"So what you mean?"

"Her hair will grow back."

"When?"

"By summer."

Trina went up, got her bag, and said, "We ready?"

Cleo said, "Uhhh."

He couldn't believe eyes. "Trina, I like the new do."

"Thanks."

Ken grabbed Trina's arm when he came in the door. "What the hell, Trina?"

"Man, if you don't remove your hand off me, it's going to be a problem."

He let Trina go, saying, "Wait until you have this baby."

"Kenneth, no, you wait."

"And you two getting married on Friday?"

Trina said, "Yes, I can't wait to become Mrs. Brown," smiling. "Where's my phone at, Kenneth?"

"Here." He handed it to her. "Tell that mother fucker stop calling you."

"Who?"

"Chris, that's who."

Trina laughed. "That's not Chris, fool. That's my aunt's number."

"Everybody's ready, so we can go."

"Yes, let's go home."

Trina told Ken, "I've been ready since I got here. And you need to stop to get a tree on our way home."

"Trina, can't we do it tomorrow?"

"No. Christmas Eve is tomorrow."

"If that will make you happy and wipe that mug off your face, we will stop and get a tree."

It was a quiet ride all the way home for the both of them.

That evening after getting home, the fellas wanted to play ball at the gym. So Kenneth told Trina he was going out for a while.

"Can you stop and get me an orange soda, please?"

"I'll think about it," he replied as he walked out the bedroom. "Wait until I get back home, and I'll help you with the tree."

"No, your ass be back late. Fuck that shit, waiting on you. Christmas be here and gone waiting on you."

Ken asked for a kiss, but Trina said, "No, I'm still pissed at you from the New York trip."

"Was I mad when Zena was eating that ass? Look, I'm out! You been trippin' since you got pregnant, and the fucked up thing is, I can't say shit. I'm out, Catrina."

"Don't forget my soda."

"Bye, Trina."

At the gym, Mitch and his crazy brother, Mikey, also came out to play ball.

Kenneth asked, "Who's the other team that wanted to play ball with us."

"Some clowns," Cleo said to Kenneth. "Let's go. Ken, who tights you got on?"

"Mine's, you fuck face."

Trent said, "I thought they were Trina's."

"She don't dress me. I dress her ass." He looked up to see Chris putting on his sneakers.

Chris went, "Dude, why the hell you didn't tell me he was going to be playing today?"

"Chris," Buddy said, "I didn't know he was playing."

"Well, well, well, if it isn't Mr. Blanks."

One guy knew Kenneth and said, "Congratulations on the baby."

"Thank you, man. Stop pass 'cause I'm getting married Friday. My mom's having a little something at the house for us."

"We playing ball or what," Chris said all rude, holding the ball.

"So you must can play since you rushing everyone."

"I can wipe you cute ass."

Ken smiled. "Let's put a wager down." He went in his bag and got his wallet. "I have six hundred, so what's up?

Chris said, "I got five hundred. Randy, spot me one hundred until we leave. It's time to shut this bitch up."

"I got your bitch," said Ken, grabbing his dick.

"You dressed like a bitch."

Kenneth was looking fly in his red tights and white shorts overtop, matching his red high- tops sneakers. Kenneth laughed. "But these my shit with my name on this brand. Can you say that, mother fucker?

Trina's brother showed up with Mel, and Kenneth and Chris were still going at it.

Mikey said, "Okay, chill, let's play ball. The game goes to twenty-one."

Ken said, "I'm ready."

It was a very intense game.

Kenneth talking shit to Chris about Trina. He said, "You're such a pussy." Kenneth smiled with the ball and was ready to piss him off even more.

Chris began blocking him, all in his face, and out of nowhere, Ken gave Chris a big kiss on the face. It shocked him so bad. Then Ken shot a three pointer in the basket.

"Chris, I go crazy when I smell pussy."

He went charging at Kenneth.

"Man, chill, you don't want none of this. I'll take this six hundred and give to my baby for a nice dress for our wedding on Friday."

"Let me go, Randy, I'm tired of his bullshit. Trust and believe you won't be with Trina long before she leaves your no-good ass."

"Hey, you may be right, but guess what? Until I die or she dies, we will have a bond between us. We'll be in each other's lives forever. And guess what? She will never divorce me, baby."

"Whatever, Kenneth. Yo, Cleo, take your boy out of here before I fuck him up."

Ken jumps over the bench and hit Chris across the face.

Mitch said, "Come on you two. Stop. Cut it out."

Mikey told Mitch to stay out of it. "Let them fight."

Cleo said, "Go for it since this is long overdue."

So they got to throwing punches. Ken was a cocky fucker and always fought dirty. He also was a black belt. But Chris was getting it in with a few licks to Kenneth's ribs. Kenneth kicked the wind out of Chris and was about to stomp him, when Cleo pushed Kenneth.

"That's enough."

Kenneth grabbed his bag, holding his side. "I'll see your punk ass around.

Cleo said, "Bro, go home," walking him outside. "Now tell me how you're going to explain this to Trina's crazy ass?"

"I'm not."

"You really don't think she's not going to find out about this shit? And they were recording it. Go home, bro. You need to go check your side out."

"Nope. I'm good."

Ken got in his truck and went on home.

Trina was in the kitchen making a cheese cake and fixing all the side dishes for Christmas dinner.

"I dressed the tree."

"It's real pretty, baby."

"Kenneth, where is my soda?"

"Oh, damn, I forgot. Can you call Timmy? He was playing ball with us and he can bring you one by."

"That's okay. What's wrong with you?"

"Nothing."

"Don't tell me nothing."

He went up and took his shirt off. His side was hurting bad.

Trina went upstairs and saw his side all bruised.

Trina asked Kenneth, "What the fuck happened?"

"Nothing, baby, I'm fine. Now can you please just run some hot bath water?"

"Look at your hands, Ken."

"I'm okay."

She told him go in the bathroom. "You stink. Babe, I like how you show me love."

"I was playing ball, Trina. That's why I stink. This dick don't stink. Bullshit."

She went back downstairs and Shelly called.

"Hey, boo."

"What's up, girl?"

"Why in the hell was Chris and Ken fighting at the gym?"

"What are you talking about?"

"Girl, go on World Star on the Internet."

"Okay."

Trina hung up and looked at the video. Trina yelled Kenneth's name so loud, he knew it was going to be a long night. She walked all up in the bathroom. Kenneth was sitting in the tub, soaking.

"Kenneth, what happened to you tonight?"

"Baby, nothing."

Trina played the video and said, "Let me refresh your little brain. Man, you were fighting with Chris."

"Look, he started in on me, Trina."

"Listen to you right now. Fighting about what, Ken?"

"Baby, he kept talking shit to me, so I had to show him what I was about. He just mad because I called him a pussy and took his damn money playing ball."

Trina was so mad with Ken.

He got out of the tub, and Trina asked if he was in pain.

"Get dress so we can go to the hospital."

Ken got dressed, and they went straight to the emergency room.

"Trina, I'm sorry about New York."

"Ken, I really don't want to talk about New York ever again."

"You love me, Trina Brown."

"Ken, I love you, but the more you pull this shit, I'll fall out of love with you."

"Trina, don't give up on us, not now."

"When you're alone with me, you're like a different person, Ken. You really need to be this way all the time. Stop trying to be this big bad dude, but really behind closed doors, you're a mama's boy."

"Trina, don't make me laugh."

He was called in the back, and Trina went with him.

Ken didn't like needles, and that was the first they wanted to do, draw his blood. He cursed and Trina said, "Man up, Kenneth. Take it like a man."

"I'll remember that when you're in labor."

Ken went down for x-rays. Trina called Chris up.

He said, "*What, Trina!*"

"What, my ass. And don't yell at me."

"Look, you called my phone. Shouldn't you be hugged up with your man?"

"What the hell you and Kenneth fighting about?"

"Nothing much. Just Ken talking shit. Why? He came crying to you?"

"I saw the video."

"Trina, we done?"

"I guess so."

Chris hung up on her.

The transporter brought Ken back and said, "The doctor should be in soon."

"Thank you."

"Hope you feel better, Mr. Brown."

"Me too." He smiled at the little lady. He then looked at Trina. "What now?"

"You just so fresh, Kenneth."

"Baby, she's our mothers' age."

He had a cracked rib, and Trina cussed his ass out. "How dumb are you, Kenneth?"

"I should have stomped his ass when I had the chance."

"Christmas Eve is tomorrow, and you can't even move."

"I bet I can move around in you tonight."

"Boy, bye!"

Walking to get the truck, a guy was standing with his friends, and they laughed at Trina and Ken.

Trina yelled, "Stay your ass over here."

"Yes, dear. Man, you married?"

"Hell no!"

"Yo smart because this the shit you need to go through."

"Trina, what you doing?"

"Ken, get in the truck."

"Trina, don't drive my baby like that."

"Fuck this truck."

"Okay, remember that when you need to drive my truck again."

"Don't worry. I'll get a truck of my own."

"Trina, you always talking trash."

Trina stopped by her mom's and got the heating pad for Ken.

Chris was sitting on his car outside. He gave Trina the finger.

Ken put the window down and yelled, "Hey, you forgot mother fucker."

Chris laughed and yelled back. "You want some more, pretty boy?"

"Sure do." Ken got out with his gun and shot at Chris.

Trina screamed so loud that her father came out running. "Trina, go in the house. *Now!*" Chris, go in your house too."

"Mr. Jones, he came at me."

"Did you not just give my wife the finger?"

"Your wife?" Trina's dad said.

Ken said, "Shit."

"You wish Trina was your wife."

"She will be real soon."

"Ken, take your ass in the house."

"I'll see you real soon."

"I'll be waiting, pretty boy. Trina Jones or is it Brown yet?

"Ken, you have a big mouth. Wait until your mom finds out about this."

"What the fuck, Trina!"

"Daddy, please don't be mad."

"I'm not mad, but I'm disappointed in both of you that neither one of you could tell us about y'all already being married."

"Daddy, we did it in North Carolina."

"Wait, so y'all been married for almost a month?"

"Yes, sir, and there's something else."

"What, Trina?"

"I'm pregnant. I'm eight weeks."

He said, "Wow!"

"Mr. Billy, we're telling everyone at Christmas on Friday. We want to do this right, so my father's going to marry us."

"Okay, we'll do it your way, but if you two keep something like this from us again, I promise you both, it won't be pretty."

Trina's mom came in the house with more bags from where she had been shopping.

"Lena, don't spend no more of my damn money."

"Man, hush. Hey, baby."

"Hi, Mommy. Well, I need to get Ken home. He has a cracked rib from fighting with Chris earlier."

"Ken, it's time to stop the bullshit, and you know what I'm talking about."

"Yes, sir, I hear you."

"Let that shit go. You with her now, fuck him."

"Let's go, Kenneth, and please just go get in the truck."

"Okay, baby, let's go home."

They walked out the door, got in the truck, and went home.

"Your dad took it pretty well."

"Ken, why would you say anything?"

"I was mad, Trina."

She pulled in the driveway and said, "Let's go." Trina hurried up and gave him a pain pill that knocked him out.

She just finished cooking when Greg came over, and Trina talked to him for a while. Then they headed over to Christine's and got the ham.

When Trina got back in the house, Ken was awake.

"Where you been, baby?"

"Getting the ham from Christine's."

"Come to bed."

"I'm coming, Ken."

"I'm still mad you cut your hair," he said.

"Get over it." Trina looked at Ken lying in the bed holding his dick, stroking it up and down. "Kenneth Brown, you so nasty."

He was begging Trina to give him some.

"Ken, what I get if I give you some cookies?"

"Some good old ice cream." He was smiling.

"No, baby, I got you. Come on," Ken said.

"I'm sorry about New York. That won't ever happen again. Now you and Zena, that can happen again. That turned me on watching y'all get busy."

Trina got in bed and told Ken that he needed to take a shower.

"Later, baby." He held his side and got on top of Trina and didn't waste no time getting busy. "After you have the baby, you should get that thing tightened so I can bust it wide open just like your first time.

"Ken, hush."

After messing around, he fell asleep and so did Trina.

The next morning Ken had to leave. He told Trina, "I'll see you this evening at your mom's."

"Okay. Where you going?"

"To Delaware. I got to pick up something."

"I don't want to know."

"Baby, it's not nothing like that."

"Yeah, okay, Kenneth."

Trina wrapped all her gifts and put them under the tree. Trina went to her shop to do some last-minute work, and Chris came by, banging on the glass door. She went out and saw him.

"Chris, what the hell are you doing?"

"Open the door, Trina. I'll bust this bitch open."

She opened the door and asked, "Are you crazy?"

"No. Are you, Trina? Where did we go wrong, Trina?"

"I don't know, Chris. I just want us to move on with our lives."

"I'm moving to Miami in a couple months so you won't need to worry about seeing me anymore. I have a job, more money, and my chance of owning my own company. Can you please keep in touch with me?" he asked. "Trina, tell me and I'll walk away and never come at you wrong again. Do you love Kenneth?"

"Yes."

"Well, are you in love with him, Trina? Answer me, Trina!"

"Yes, I do."

Chris told her, "I don't believe you at all. I do know that you're still in love with me." He backed her against the wall and kissed her lips. "I tell you what, I'll back off now, but when you ready to settle down and have a talk about us, let me know." He went in his pocket and pulled out a box with pink diamond earrings inside and a card with cash in it.

"Chris, I can't take this."

"You can and you will. You can marry this man, and you can have babies by him, but I know you still love me. Merry Christmas, Trina."

"Merry Christmas, Christopher."

Trina sat there for a little bit, then went home.

Ken said, "Baby, you home?"

"Yes, I am."

"Okay, put your coat on and walk outside."

"Ken, I'm cooking."

"I'm going to help you. Just come outside."

"Okay."

Trina got her coat, and he pulled up, blowing the horn of a black Mercedes Benz truck.

Trina said, "Oh my God! Kenneth, that's nice."

"Merry Christmas, baby."

"This is mine?"

"Yes, it is. Do you like it?"

"I love it.

"Don't put down the windows. They just got done being tinted."

She got inside and began to cry.

"Oh, Lawd, Trina, please don't cry."

"Thank you, husband."

He was so pumped. "Look, baby, it has a TV for junior when he get older."

"It may be a girl, Kenneth."

"Your dad went with us, and he loves this truck, Trina."

"I bet he does. Ken, I don't know what to say."

"Say you love me and we're going to have lots of babies."

"How many babies?"

"As many as you can have."

"I was thinking about two kids, Ken."

"Okay, two will do for now."

They went back inside, and Trina called her father.

"Baby girl, you like it?" he asked.

"Oh, Daddy, yes, yes, it is beautiful."

"Your mom loves it, and now she wants one."

"Tell Mommy, we'll work on that."

"She heard you over her, smiling."

"Well, Ken and me are ready to start baking these other pies."

"Okay, see you for breakfast, baby girl."

"Yes, sir, we'll be there."

"Ken, your mom called. I talked to her already, and she just wanted to know what time dinner is gonna start. I told her at four o'clock."

Ken was a pretty good cook. He sat down and helped Trina make the pies from scratch. He even mixed up the crabmeat.

"Damn, how much this costing us? Your mom fixing the pig feet, right?"

"Yes, Kenneth, and Aunt Betty fixing ribs and frying chicken."

"That's what I'm talking about."

Trina fixed the big pan of seafood salad.

Ken said, "Damn, baby, that taste good," and got a bowl to help himself to some more.

Trina sat down and ate a sandwich with a big glass of milk.

"Baby, don't you get tired of eating?"

"No. Get the pies, Ken."

Cleo called, telling Ken to open the door.

"Baby, get the door, it's Cleo," Trina said.

"Hey, Cleo,"

"What up, sis?"

"Nothing. Ken's in the kitchen."

"Bro, Trina got you baking?"

"Yes, keep it to yourself. I need some help with the beer and wine."

Trina said, "I know I'm drinking some of that tomorrow. One glass though."

"Why one glass, Ken?"

"Cleo, I'm pregnant."

"For real?"

"Yes, and the news will be out tomorrow after dinner. Ken, go ahead and tell him you then spilled the bean already."

"When we went away to North Carolina, we got married."

"No, you didn't."

"Yes, we did."

"Yo, bro, why you didn't tell me?"

"We wanted to do it here for everyone, Cleo. Man, don't be mad. Tomorrow, I want you to stand up for me as my best man."

"Tomorrow?" Trina said,

"Baby, why not? Since everyone will be here."

"I would love to, bro," Cleo said as they hugged. "So in New York, y'all was already married?"

"Yes. We're going to wait until the baby's born, then we're going on a long honeymoon before I go away."

That next day was stressful for Trina.

Ken said, "Baby, so the drinks for the game are downstairs?"

"I put some in the fridge in the kitchen."

"You okay?"

"Yes, baby, chill. Everything looks great."

People started arriving at the house. Kenneth's parents came along with his lil' bro, Kent, and his girl. Trina even invited Mitch and Lisa for Christmas dinner. And Ken was fine with that. They opened gifts from under the tree.

Trina said, "Here, this is for you and Lisa. I hope you both like it."

"Thanks, Trina. Nice house."

"Thanks."

Ken welcomed Lisa, and she asked, "You buying?"

"No, we renting, but we're remodeling a house in Atlanta that Trina's grandfather owned and was left to Trina. It's being worked on now."

Trina said, "Yes, we'll use it as a summer home until Ken finish up in Japan."

"Next year this time, I'll be leaving for Japan for a few months, coming back home for a couple months and then return to Japan for six more months. I'll be home for good after that."

Everybody arrived, and Trina's had her truck parked outside.

"Whose truck?"

"It's mine. My Christmas gift from Ken."

"Where the keys at?" asked Ken.

"Hanging up in the kitchen, Dad."

"Trina, you cooked all this food?"

"Most of it, with Kenneth's help."

"Shhh, baby, don't tell everybody I be in the kitchen cooking."

"Why not? You want to open up a restaurant one day."

"I know, but I won't be cooking."

"Everyone, the food's ready. Mama Lena, where's my pot at?"

"On the stove. I put some in the fridge too."

"Thank you."

"Baby, sit down, and I'll fix your plate. You been going all day."

"Okay, okay, I'm sitting, Ken."

He fixed her a plate.

"Ken, that's too much food," she said.

"Trina, your greedy ass be eating more than that at night. Eat, please," he said, kissing her on the nose.

"Tia, you need to taste the seafood salad. Mitch, no ribs?"

"No, thanks, I don't eat meat."

"Lisa, you meat free also?"

"Yes."

"That's why you so damn boney." He laughed.

"Ken, you're a mess, I tell you. And, Trina, this salad is really good."

"Thanks. Hey, Shelly, where the eggs at? Kenneth, I don't want this. I want egg rolls, rice, an egg, and some sweet potatoes. Where's the crab cakes?"

He took her plate. Timmy fixed Trina a plate.

"Why you being so nice, brother?"

"No reason. I got your gift you asked for." He got to smiling.

"Oh my Lawd, who made the potato salad?"

"What's wrong?" Ken asked.

"Man, it's the bomb!"

Trina laughed and told him that Kenneth made it.

"Bro, you holding out on me?"

"No, not at all. Look, my nana told me don't wait on no woman to cook for your ass. So I watched her and my mom cook. When Mrs. Thing tell me she's not cooking, I have three choices— my parent's house, the Jones's house, or fix it my damn self."

Everyone got done eating by the time Trent got there.

"Hello, everyone."

"It's about time."

Everyone headed down to the basement, and it was huge.

Mr. Brown stood up. "Can I have everyone's attention?"

Ken went in the closet, and he handed Cleo one box. He took Trina's hands in his.

"Trina, I have told you this more than once. I have wanted you to be my lady since college. I love you so much. Today I ask you in front of our family and friends, will you marry me?"

"Yes."

He slipped the ring on her finger. "Now I asked you, will you marry me today, right here, right now."

Her mom said, "Oh my Lawd, girl, you go ahead get your man."

Everyone laughed.

"Yes, Kenneth, today with our love and everyone here to witness it." She looked at her dad, smiling.

He winked at her.

Trina stood with her dad, who gave her away. Ken's mom, Gwen, and Trina's mom, Lena, cried, holding each other's hand as their children said their wedding vows. Mitch was standing, holding his wife, Lisa, around the waist.

"This is amazing," she said.

They said their "I do's," and Kenneth kissed Catrina like never before.

"Ken, son, come up for air."

"Love you, wifey."

"Love you, husband."

"Parents, I need you to open your gifts."

They did.

Trina's mom screamed, "I'm going to be a grandmother."

His mom was so happy.

Shelly and Christine were going to be aunts.

"Greg, you ready to be an uncle/godfather to our baby?"

"Yes." He hugged Trina.

"I'm eight weeks today."

Wait, so you and Ken did the damn thang?"

Ken teased, "She wanted it so bad."

"Mama Lena, you remember when you two went to Virginia?"

"Yes, say no more."

"Ken, you talking too much."

"Oh Lawd," Trina's father said. "Thank you for making Trina go to college and thank you for moving her out my house."

"Okay, everyone, you can open your gifts now or take them home with you."

The guys sat downstairs and talked some more. Trina sat down looking at the rings that she couldn't wait to wear. Ken came upstairs.

"Baby, what you doing?"

"Looking at my ring."

"Now you can wear it. Do you need some help?"

Mitch and Lisa came up to say congratulations and thank you for letting them be a part of their special day.

"Trina, call me at the studio soon."

"Okay, I have something big coming up in June."

"Okay, let me know 'cause I'm down for LA, baby."

"Oh, really?"

"Yes, so do everything the doctors say and we can do this."

"I will." Trina walked them out.

"Hey, Trina's pies. Cleo, take them downstairs, please."

The ladies helped Trina fix a platter with food on it, and they put everything away, sitting out the desserts on the counter.

"Mommy, you okay?"

"Yes. I'm going to be a grandmother." She smiled.

"Yes, Mommy. And this time he or she will be okay."

They hugged each other. Trina had a small glass of wine. Ken told her drink it slow.

"Yes, Daddy."

The fellas sat downstairs, yelling, watching football while Trina and the ladies sat upstairs talking about life.

"I should have known something. Every time I talked to Kenneth and asked what were you doing, he would say eating or lying down."

"Yes, my medicine makes me sleep."

"Trina, what the doctors say about you taking medicine while being pregnant?"

Well, it's a 50/50 chance that I'll have the baby early, but Ken has hired a team of doctors to watch the baby and I very closely. We'll pray that everything will be okay."

As time went on, Trina was doing very well carrying the baby. She decided to go to LA with Mitch to do his new CD. Ken told Trina that he couldn't drive out and that he had a lot of business to deal with, so he would be there on Friday night in time for the show. They rode off in the RV going there.

Trina said, "See, this why we flying back. I can't do all this riding in a RV?" She lay down.

Mitch said to Trina, "You okay?"

"Yes, I'm fine. What's up?"

"I just don't understand why Ken didn't come along with you."

"He'll be here tonight."

"Well, we're almost there anyway so take a nap until we get there."

Mitch told Mac that he hopes Ken's not doing no dumb shit.

"Like what?"

Mitch looked at Mac.

"You really think so?"

"Man, I told you, I saw Ken with some chick one night, and it wasn't even Trina. I didn't tell her. Only because she's pregnant and I don't want to upset her."

"Let's hope he's not because he knows Trina's crazy."

Arriving in LA, Trina was ready to eat, shower, and chill. Ken got there just in time as Trina was about to sing. She waved at him and he waved as he held flowers for Trina. After the show, Ken walked back to greet his wife, kissing her and kissing her belly. They went out for a walk and later relaxed in their hotel room that night. Ken had turned his phone off, telling her it was all about her tonight.

First thing in the morning, Trina met up with Mitch and said, "We're about to leave to get home. Good luck tonight, Mitch. Blow them away."

"I'll sing for you and me."

Mitch had two more shows to do before coming home.

Trina and Ken went back home, but they had to make a stop first. He had planned a baby shower for Trina at the park. She had a great time, but she was ready to go home. She was beat.

Ken said that he was leaving out for a few and would see her in a bit, kissing her goodbye.

Part 2

Trina was lying on the sofa looking at TV when Greg walked in with the rest of the cake and gifts, saying, "Trina, who does that?"

"What, Greg?" she asked.

"Leaves their own baby shower?"

"Greg, I was tired," she replied.

Trina's phone rang, and it was Lynn.

"Hey, girl, what's up?"

She told Trina, "I'm at the hotel, and you need to go to room 311. I just saw Kenneth and some girl."

"Okay. Thanks, Lynn," Trina told. "Greg, let's go."

"Where, Trina?" he asked.

Walking to the truck, she gave Greg her wallet with her bank cards. "If I need to be bailed out of jail, my pin is Mommy's birthday."

Driving as fast as she could to the hotel, Trina yelled, "Mother fucker, sorry bitch!" She grabbed her phone and called Ken, but he didn't answer. Trina told Greg, "I'll be right back." She went to the room and knocked on the door.

The girl opened the door, and Trina said, "Hello, bitch! I'm wifey," and went in on her ass.

Greg went running into the room.

Ken heard yelling and jumped out the shower. He came out and saw Trina beating the chick that he was with.

Greg grabbed Trina off the girl. "Trina, the baby, it's not worth it. Let's go. Ken, man, come on. Your wife's pregnant, and you up in the hotel with a bitch!"

"So, Kenneth, this what you cheating on me with?"

He tried to explain to Trina, but she wasn't trying to hear nothing he had to say.

When Trina and Greg walked out, Kenneth said, "Why the fuck would your dumb ass open the door?"

"Kenneth, you never said you had a wife."

"Bitch! I don't need to let you know shit," he said as he put his clothes on.

Trina went downstairs to get her bat out the back seat that she kept for shit like this.

Greg looked and said, "Oh shit!"

Trina told Greg, "Get in the truck now!"

Greg tried to talk her out of busting his truck up, but Trina went to town with her bat.

"You want to fuck with me!" She bust every window out Kenneth's truck, then went into her truck and got a screwdriver and flattened all the tires.

A man that was in the next room banged on the door, and Ken came out, asking, "Was that my truck?" Kenneth looked and said, "Fuck, Trina!"

She then yelled, "Fuck you and that bitch!"

Trina and Greg got in her truck and went to her house.

Greg called Trina's dad and told him, "It's about to get ugly."

Her father asked, "What happened now, Greg?"

"Well, Trina just bust Ken's windows out his truck at a hotel."

"What! Please just get to the house."

"You know she crazy, Pop," Greg said. "Trina, why you holding your stomach?"

"Greg, not now, please."

She went upstairs and called Ken's dad. He didn't even get to say hello. All he heard was Trina crying and telling him to come get Ken's things because he can't stay here anymore.

"Trina, what's going on?"

"Ken's a liar, a cheater, and I want him gone." She sighed. She started grabbing his clothes out the closet and stuffing them in his duffle bags and throwing some out the window.

Trina's brother came to her house looking around and said, "What the fuck's going on, Greg?"

He tried to explain from what he saw at the hotel.

Trina stopped and rushed to the phone calling the 1-800 number, reporting her bank card to her accounts were missing and to please stop all transactions until she comes to the bank in the morning. The bank put a freeze on her accounts, which really belonged to Kenneth. She hung up the phone, mumbling, "He wanna fuck with me!"

Trina's dad pulled up and saw all Kenneth's clothes on the lawn packed up. He told Trina to go sit down.

"Daddy, he had a girl at a hotel, and you want me to sit down? No, Daddy, not this time. I'm tired of his bullshit, and it will take a long time for me to want to be with his cheating ass again."

Cleo's truck pulled in as Kenneth's father and brother, Kent, pulled up.

Cleo said, "Man, she's pissed."

"Cleo, I fucked up," Ken stated, "didn't I?

"Bro, you think?"

"I know," he said, "I can't even be mad right now."

"Man, Trina's crazy ass put all your shit outside on the lawn."

Ken and Cleo got out the truck.

Ken asked Trina, "Could I please come inside to get my computer?"

"Hell no!" she replied. "Kent, can you please go in the house and get your brother's laptop from the office?"

"Trina, can I go in the office cause I need to get my money?"

She told Ken, "Please don't put your feet on the steps."

"Trina, I also live here too, okay?"

As he start walking toward her, she rushed inside the house and called 911, telling the operator, "Yes, my husband and I aren't getting along, and I asked him to leave the house. I'm scared for my life, and I'm pregnant. Could someone please hurry?" Trina went downstairs and told Ken to get out of the house.

He said, "Trina, some of my money's gone."

"What do you want from me, Ken? Get out!" Trina pointed the gun at him, saying, "Get out of my house now!"

"Trina, don't point that gun at me."

She fired it, and he ducked.

I said, "Get out my house now!"

He got his stuff, and as he came out, he looked back at her. "I can't believe you called the fucking cops on me," he said.

The police car was pulling up when he came outside. He yelled, "Really, Trina!"

Cleo was putting everything inside the truck. He said, "Kenneth, take your ass down the street."

"See, this why I can't wait to go over to Japan to get away from that mouth."

"Yes, please do make me some money," Trina replied.

Ken looked at her and couldn't say nothing.

"Yeah, remember whatever you do, you answer to me. I'm that bitch you'll never forget." Trina put the gun in the draw before she opened the door for the cops. "Could you please just stay here until he gets all his things, please?"

"Yes, that's our plan, ma'am."

One officer told Ken, "Come in the house and get whatever you need until she cools off."

Ken went upstairs and got his bag from the bathroom. While doing all that, Ken's mom had called the house.

"Mom, you need to talk to Trina. She's here playing the victim, and she bust my truck up and tossed my clothes outside."

"Kenneth, you have a son coming, and this what you want to show him?"

"No, Mom."

"Well then, get your shit together, and I'll see you in a few."

Ken went back down to the living room and looked at Trina. She was so mad and had hate in her eyes. He went on out the door.

"Billy, can you please get Trina to go to the house tonight. Or, Greg, please take her to your house. I don't want her staying alone at night."

"I'll take her to my house, Ken."

"Thanks, Greg. Tell her I fucked up and I'm sorry."

Greg said, "Ken, stop pass the shop tomorrow. I want to talk to you."

"Yes, sir, I will."

The cops went to their cars and waited until Ken left.

Greg went in and said, "Okay, pack a bag, and come to the house with me. Ken doesn't want you to stay alone."

"Greg, I'll be fine."

"No, Trina, pack a bag. Cut me some cake, please."

While Trina went upstairs and picked out some out clothes, her dad came up and asked, "Baby girl, you okay?"

"Yes, sir, I'm just so tired."

"I know you are. You're so like your mom," he replied. "It takes a strong woman to teach us right from wrong. It took me a couple years to learn what I was missing at home."

"Chris was right, Dad. He was going to lie, cheat, and break my heart. And he has. But, Daddy, I will be okay. I'm going to have my baby and move to Atlanta."

Then Greg came and got her bag.

Trina grabbed her stomach, praying, "*Don't you have this baby.*"

"Trina!"

"I'm fine, Greg, let's go."

Trina's dad locked up the house after grabbing her meds off the table. Walking to the truck, her father said, "Take your meds."

"Thanks. I need this to sleep tonight."

*****

Trina went to Greg's house, and she tried to relax but couldn't. She went in the room with Greg and lay on his bed, talking half the night. She finally went to sleep.

Trina got up, then woke Greg up. She was crying.

"Trina, please tell me you peed on yourself or something?"

"No," she said. "Greg, the baby can't come now. He just can't."

"I'm ready to call Kenneth, right now."

Trina said, "Please don't call him."

Greg said, "Look, Trina, I know you mad with him but put that aside."

"Okay, just hurry please, 'cause I'm still peeing on myself."

Greg called Kenneth, and he answered, saying, "Trina, I'm not trying to fight this morning."

"Ken, it's Greg."

"Hey, what's up?"

"Trina's water broke. I'm ready to help her get cleaned up. and then we're going to the hospital. I'll call her doctor and be on my way to your house."

Kenneth could hear Trina crying in the background. When Ken hung up, he slipped on some clothes and ran out the house. He didn't even wake up anyone in the house to tell them anything.

Greg got her into the shower, and Trina was a hot mess. Greg was so done with her. After bathing, she got out.

All Greg kept saying was, "Trina, please don't have the baby on my watch."

Ken beat her parents to the house and was banging on the front door.

"Now listen to this dumb fuck waking up everyone on the block."

Trina was yelling and leaning over the bed.

Ken asked, "Where's Trina?"

"She's in the room."

He went back to the room and saw Trina was in a towel.

Kenneth asked, "Where's your bag, Trina?"

"On the floor," she whispered.

Ken said, "I'll get her dressed, Greg." Then Kenneth picked Trina up and carried her out to his truck.

Greg got her purse and said, "Let's go."

Ken told Trina, "I need you to inhale and exhale, okay?"

"He can't come yet, it's too early," Trina cried.

"Trina, he is coming, okay? We got this." Ken buckled her in the seat, and he and Greg got in the truck and pulled off.

Her father was racing in to turn, but he saw Kenneth, so he turned back around to follow them to the hospital.

Ken got to the hospital first, pulling right in front the doors and getting Trina out of the truck. He went inside, yelling, "I need some help. My wife is in labor."

The nurse came with a wheelchair.

Greg asked Kenneth for his car keys. "I need to move the truck inside the garage."

Ken went rushing into the back area and told the nurses his wife's water had broken about twenty-five minutes ago. "She's seven months pregnant, and here's all her paperwork. I already called her doctor."

"He's here, Mr. Brown."

The nurse looked so scared that Trina asked her, "What wrong?"

When she got on the bed, she said, "I can feel him, Ken."

Ken said, "Hey, somebody better get her doctor. I see my son's hair."

They called stat for the doctor.

Trina started pushing until she pushed his little head out.

Ken said, "Uhhhh, shit!"

The nurse grabbed some gloves as Trina yelled get him out and baby boy came sliding out onto the bed. The nurse used the suction to clear his airways and started rubbing and tapping his lil' behind.

"Come on, little fella," the nurse said.

Her doctor came in and picked the baby up, massaged his little chest, and he then began to cry.

"Take him now to NICU, right now!"

Ken held Trina in his arms, and they both cried.

The doctor told Trina, "I need to ask you to give me one big push," as he pressed down on her stomach.

The nurse came back and got Kenneth.

The doctor said to Trina, "You have one stitch." Her doctor told the nurse, "Please get me her mom."

Trina was so upset that her mom had to help clean her up. "Greg is on his way with everything, Trina."

They had to give Trina some medicine to calm her nerves. She was so upset.

Ken was standing there holding his son, who was five pounds and three ounces and so beautiful.

"We have a lot of test to do, Mr. Brown."

"Please do every test there is for my newborn son. Trina wasn't that big when she was carrying him."

"Well, he's five pounds, three ounces and sixteen inches long."

"He's short like his mom."

The nurse laughed.

"I need to go tell my wife what's going on."

"She's asleep now because the doctor gave her something to sleep and calm her down."

"Good." Ken got to hold his son for another minute before they placed the oxygen mask over his face. Ken left and went back to Trina's room to tell her their son weighed five pounds, he's small, and his short ass is sixteen inches long. He suggested to "Go see him before they start all his test."

Ken hugged Trina's parents. He walked over and said, "Trina."

She opened her eyes started to cry.

Ken said, "No, Trina. He's okay at five pounds and three ounces."

"Oh, Ken, I want to see him."

"Okay."

Greg walked in with her bag. Ken asked if Trina wanted him to help her.

"I guess so," Trina replied.

He helped her into the bathroom and sat her down.

"Trina, I know I fucked up really bad, and I'm trying to fix our marriage."

"How many women are there, Kenneth?"

"Trina..." he said.

"No, I want to know. I do not want to be blindsided, so tell me."

"I've been seeing a couple women, Trina. But they don't mean nothing to me, Trina."

"So what, I'm not enough for you that you had to go out and have random female to fuck?"

"Trina, no, I don't know what I was thinking."

"This can't be happening to me. You promise to be there for me and our child."

"Trina, I will fix it. I'll do anything. I just want to be with you and our son."

Trina said, "Can we go see our son, please. I can't do this right now. But I'll tell you this right here, right now. You end all this, and, if not, I will pack up and move to Atlanta. And you will never see your son ever again. Now move out of my way and take me to see KJ." Trina walked out the bathroom and asked, "Are you coming, Kenneth?"

"Yes."

Trina sat in the wheelchair, and Ken said to Greg, "You going down?"

"In a few. I'm waiting for Shelly and Christine to come upstairs."

Ken said, "Okay." He took Trina to see their son.

He was lying there with his eyes open.

Trina got up and said, "Hello, KJ. I'm your mommy. Boy, you look like your father."

The nurse asked if she wanted to feed him.

"Yes, can I, please?"

Trina was given a bottle to she feed her baby. She was smiling so hard while looking at him. Trina kissed him and told her baby, "You have a mommy that loves you so much."

"My son has gray eyes."

"Yes, I can see that. I'll pray for him that he won't act like you when he gets older, Trina."

"I will also."

"Look, I need to go take care of some things, grab a bag, and I will be back. I'll stop and get you something to eat too."

Kenneth left, went to the house, and grabbed some clothes. One of his tricks called and said, "Congratulations on your son."

"Thanks."

"Now that he's here, bring that good dick over here and please me like the last time."

He told her, "Look, I need to be with my family. That means more to me than a piece of pussy that belongs to another man."

"Kenneth, so what now, you telling me you need to be with that bitch of a wife of yours?"

He turned around, saying, "Where you at?"

"I'm at home."

"I am on my way."

Kenneth called his other bitch and told her he wouldn't be seeing her anymore. "I need to man up as a husband and father."

She wasn't mad. She wished him well and said, "Kenneth, please grow up for your family. You owe that to the both of them." Then she hung up the phone.

When Mr. Brown got to ole girl place and she opened the door, he grabbed her by the hair and said, "Let me tell you something. You know nothing about my wife. She never did anything to deserve what I have done. So the next time you form your lips, it better be sucking my dick if I need a good blow. Other than that, don't you ever talk about my wife again. You got it?"

"Yes," she replied. "Now let my arm go, you're hurting me."

"Bitch, you lucky that's all I did." He opened the door and said, "Sandy, the pussy wasn't all that, but the dick sucking you got that down pack." He smiled and walked out the door.

All Trina's friends had come over, and she was trying to put on this happy face in front of them all. Ken walked in with his bag hanging from his shoulder and had food for the both of them. Holding flowers and a teddy bear in his hands, he handed Trina the flowers and kissed her. He whispered in her ear, "It's a wrap."

Trina looked at him.

Ken said, "I didn't know everyone was going to be here. I would have brought food for everyone."

"That's fine, Ken. We about to go have a drink for Trina."

"Well, Greg, have one for me too."

"I will, don't worry about that," he said.

"Ken, your parents said they will see you tomorrow."

"Okay, cool. Where's Billy and Mom at?" he asked.

"Mommy went to feed KJ, and Daddy went with her."

"You didn't want to feed him, Trina?"

"I was waiting on you to get back, so you could help feed him."

"Thanks. We'll eat and relax until it's time to feed the baby again."

Kenneth plugged up his laptop and phone when a knock came on the door. It was his assistant, Simms.

"Congratulations, Trina." Simms came with a gift bag and handed it to her.

Trina said, "Thank you."

"I will only be a minute." She gave Kenneth the folders.

He said, "I will be on my laptop, so email and any questions call me or text."

"Yes, sir."

He went through all the papers and signed them. "Thank you, Simms."

"Again, congrats," she said. "And, Trina, please keep him at home and not in the office."

"I'll try, Tammy."

"Now see, Trina calls me Tammy."

Ken said, "I'm your boss that's why."

"Bye!"

Everyone started leaving, and Trina began to eat her food.

Ken asked Trina, "Don't you want to know what happened?"

"No. Not at all, Kenneth." She just ate and lay back, waiting to feed her son that night.

Kenneth helped her feed and then changed his Pampers later that night.

Getting back to the room that night, after a long stay, just watching their son sleep, Ken told, Trina, "You should go lay down and get some rest."

Trina went back and lay down, and Ken asked if he could lie beside her.

She said, "Kenneth, you gotta be kidding me. You better lay your whoring ass on that sofa and think long and hard what you have done and worry how you will ever get to smell this again. Now lie on that!" She turned the overhead light off and went to sleep.

Early that morning the doctor came in and checked on Trina to see how she was doing.

Kenneth asked him how long the baby needed to stay in the hospital.

The doctor said, "A couple weeks."

Trina wasn't happy, but she knew it was for the best.

The following day she was released from the hospital, and Ken returned back to the house, going back and forth to the hospital daily with Trina to be with their son. Ken's phone only would ring if it was his parents or Cleo to check on the baby or see if they needed anything.

A couple of weeks of ripping and running back and forth, day and night, to see their child had their bodies beat. But all that had come to an end. Trina brought her son home, and she was on top of the world, just knowing he was at home. Trina's mom came to help out, knowing this wouldn't be easy having a newborn to take care of. Kenneth had to go get some things for Trina from the store since she was breastfeeding KJ.

When Ken came back, he was with Trina's brother.

Timmy yelled, "Sis, where's the runt at?"

"Timmy, stop being loud."

"Look who's talking with that big mouth. This boy better get used to a loud family while the biggest mouths are sitting in the room with him."

"Timmy, what you want?"

"Let me use your truck to go get Sherry."

"You got gas money?"

"No!"

"Well, you can't use my truck."

He looked at Ken. "Brother-in-law?"

"You know the answer to using my truck."

"Mommy, let me use your van."

"Timmy, have my van back in twenty minutes."

"Yes, ma'am."

"Trina, I hope he keeps your ass up all night."

"Boy, bye, before I call Daddy on you."

Ken had picked KJ up and went in the office and was on his video chat with his aunts, who were the wildest twins ever, showing his son off to everyone.

"Nana, as soon as Trina can travel and the doctors say Kenneth, Jr. can also, we will be to see you."

Trina came in and said, "Hello, everyone." She promised to bring the baby to see them soon. Trina then took him so she could feed him.

Trina said, "Mommy, he won't take my boob."

"Trina, he will. Just take your time.

"Look, little boy, you need to eat.

Ken came out, asking, "What, he won't eat?"

"No, he's showing off."

"Trina, he's used to the bottle. You pumped some in a bottle yet?"

"Yes."

Ken went to get the bottle, and KJ took to it easily.

Trina sat and fed him. "Mommy, I will be okay. If I need you, best believe, I'll be calling you."

Ken said, "I will be back. I need to run to the house."

He wasn't gone long at all. He went and got some more clothes and took up to the room.

"Trina, I can stay in the room, can't I?"

She just looked at him and said, "Ken, just stay on your side, and everything will be fine up in here."

That night the baby slept pretty good for them. Ken rolled over next to Trina, holding her closely. Trina wasn't feeling Ken at all. She was on the shot since her last checkup.

"Now, Trina, how long you're going to treat me like this?"

"I don't know, Kenneth. You tell what should I do? I mean, should I forget you cheated, more than once, twice, three times. Tell me how should I feel about this?"

"Listen, Trina. I'm sorry, and I will show you that I want our marriage to work. I fucked up, okay? Trina look at our son. Baby, come on, I leave in five months, let's make this special. When KJ gets six months, come to Japan and stay there with me until I come back to the States."

"I will see," Trina said. "We need to get some sleep before KJ wakes up."

Ken got up and had phone meetings all morning while Trina took care of their son.

Ken said, "Trina, I'm gonna finish. What you need me to do?"

"Can you take him while I take a nap?" she asked.

"Yes, come on, son. You want to go see granddaddy."

Trina had two bottles, four Pampers, and a sleeper for messy ass. "Tell Grandma Gwen not to rock him or hold him while he's sleeping."

Trina went upstairs and lay down after Ken left with the baby.

That night Trina and Ken were up washing bottles together.

Cleo called.

"What's going on bro?"

"We heading out to play pool."

He looked at Trina. "No, y'all go without me. I'm in for the night with KJ and wifey."

Trina said, "Ken, why don't you go out?"

"I'm okay with the baby."

"Because I choose not to, Trina." Ken held Trina gently. "I want to be with my wife." He kissed her.

Trina finally gave in and kissed him back. "Ken, stop please. You keep doing this dumb shit and my stupid ass keep falling for it over and over again." She walked away, sitting down on the chair. "I find numbers in your phone, text messages from hoes, and bitches calling my damn phone telling me you just left them. You know how that makes me feel, Kenneth. I'm your wife."

"I know that, Trina."

"Then act like it for once, Kenneth. Just once I want you to be here for me like I've been for you. It hurts, Kenneth. It hurts really bad. In the hospital, I tried to focus on our son, and all I could think about was who my husband was banging. And that's sad. I want to be loved like I deserve to be loved, not just on your arm as your beautiful wife. A woman that you love, want, and can't get enough of. That's what I want. Chris was right about you."

"About what, Trina?"

"That you would hurt me, dog me, and try to break me down. And for a while, you did. But sitting here for a few weeks, I had time to think real long and hard about us. And I decided that I can do bad by myself. So this the deal, Kenneth Brown. You want this marriage as bad as I do, then you prove it to yourself and us, meaning your wife and son. If not, I'm leaving to go down South and start another life without you and find someone that really cares about me." Trina wiped her eyes and said, "Now I am going back upstairs to feed our son."

Ken sat down again. He yelled upstairs telling Trina he was going for a walk.

She heard the door close and looked out the window as he walked toward her parents' house. Trina sat down and kissed her son.

Mitch called Trina just to check on her. She was feeling a lil' down, so he said, "Trina, if you need to talk, I'm here for you."

"Tomorrow evening, can I come to the studio to let some stress out?"

"Yes, what time?"

"I don't know, Mitch. Let's just say five o'clock."

"Okay, sounds good. I'll have Mac let you in."

"Okay, thanks, Mitch."

"Hey, anytime, Trina."

While Trina was home, Ken knocked on his in-laws door, then walked inside.

Trina's dad said, "Ken, how you get here? I didn't hear your truck pull up."

"I walked over," he replied.

"What! You walked?"

"Yes, needed some air."

"What happened?"

"Hey, Ma."

"Where's Trina."

"In the house feeding KJ's spoiled butt."

"Yes, look at the parents," she told him.

"What you cooking?" Trina called the house.

Timmy said, "What's up, sis?"

"Nothing. Ken over there?"

"Yes, He just walked in about five minutes ago. You want him?"

"No. I just was checking on him."

"What, you hurt his feelings?"

"Yes, brother. I'm tired of Ken treating me wrong."

"Hey, do what you need to do. Sis, you have the power to let him go or want him. So don't give in. Stay strong. You hold all the cards. Do his ass like Mommy did Daddy. Make him beg to come back. When he go to Japan and he returns, let him come back and you're gone. Make him miss your ass."

"I might just do that, brother. You should have been my sister, not my brother."

"Girl, bye!"

"See, you sound like me." They both laughed, Timmy said.

"Whatever. Kiss my nephew for me."

"I will."

Mr. Billy had his son-in-law out back having a drink, telling him some good shit he needed to know about Trina.

"Sit down, Ken. You need to hear this from me. Trina has been through so much. Being dogged by guys she dated. And the females didn't like her cause her hair was too long, because of the color of her skin, because she has the figure they wanted. Trina's a very smart young woman who put together a business at twenty-four years old, and she was riding in an old beat-up car, trying to open up her own business. Trina made a promise to her grandfather that she would open her shop in a year, find a man that loved her for her, and leave all these sorry fucks alone. She made this promise to him on his dying day. So when you came in her life, I seen this glow on her face I never seen before. And for my daughter to marry you without coming to Billy Jones to talk it over…she loved you and still loves you very much. Now I can't say too much because I did the same fucked up shit to her mother. I hurt her so bad, Ken. And now I still see the hurt in her eyes when I walk out the door because she still doesn't all the way trust me. When you see your woman flip what you have done to her on you, it's no joke. It's a wake-up call. So, son, I'm telling you to show her. Talk to her and let her know you're trying to fix it, however long it takes."

"Pops, I really fucked up, didn't I?"

"Yeah, you did, son. You better be getting up to KJ all night. When she get up, you better be rising also."

"Oh, Lawd!"

"Yes, you'll need him too, so keep calling on the Lawd until the Brown house is back on track. Keep hope alive, son." He laughed at Ken, who looked so sad.

Ken fixed a fish sandwich for him, and Trina and said, "Let me get home."

"Okay, Ken, remember what I said."

"Thanks, Pops."

When Ken left, Billy sat down and said, "That got damn girl got him all fucked up in the head."

"Good for her," Lena said. "Maybe he'll wake up and realize he's a married man with a child."

Trina was putting KJ to sleep, but he must had smelled his father because he started moving that little head around. Ken walked in and went up to Trina.

"Baby, your mom was fixing fish, and I brought you a sandwich back."

"Thanks."

"Son, what you doing still up? You smelled Daddy, didn't you?" Ken went to wash his hands, then took his shirt off. He told Trina, "I got him, go."

"Do you?"

He turned on the basketball game. "Okay, little fella, let's look at the game." Ken propped him on a few pillows, and his eyes got big seeing the huge TV on the wall with people running around.

Trina got in the shower, and when she came out, she looked at him. Just seeing Ken took all her pain and worries away.

"Tell Mommy that's going to be you soon."

Trina took her towel off.

Ken said, "Trina, come here for a second."

She put her robe on. “Yes.”

He sat up and put his arms around Trina, laying his head on her stomach. “I love you, Trina and don’t ever think different. I just made bad choices, and I’m going to show you the Kenneth you met.”

“I hope so, Ken. Now get your son. He just rolled over.”

“Boy, slow down.”

Trina went down and got her sandwich. “Ken, you want yours?”

“No, I’m going to take a shower. Let me know the score.”

Trina put KJ in his rocking crib and gave him his nipple. “Now go to sleep.”

Trina sent Greg, Shelly, and Christine a picture of KJ in his crib.

“Can we do lunch tomorrow?”

“Yes.”

“Greg’s restaurant?” Greg said.

“Yes, at twelve noon.”

Everyone said, “Okay.”

Ken came out the bathroom, and Trina asked him, “What time you get off tomorrow?”

“Around 3:00 p.m. Why what’s up?”

“I’m going into the studio around five o’clock, but I can have your mom watch him, if you’re going to play ball.”

“I was.”

“Call her, and I’ll pick him up around 5:30 or 6:00 p.m.”

Trina called and his grandma Gwen was excited to watch him.

“Okay, I’ll bring him around 4:30 p.m., Ma.”

“Okay.” Trina turned to Ken. “Ken, she’s excited and ready.”

“I know she would be.”

Trina called her mom to ask could she watch KJ at noon so she could go to lunch with Greg and the ladies. “Yes, I’ll bring him to you.”

"Thank you."

Kenneth said, "You need to get out. I have a business trip coming up in a few weeks in New Jersey."

Trina just looked at him.

"And I was thinking you and KJ should come with me. It's just two days and a thirty-minute ride from your aunt's. We can leave that Sunday night."

"That sounds really nice. You sure, Ken?"

"Yes. I'll be in the hotel from 8:00 to 4:00 p.m., and I can get the meeting over by 2:30 p.m. Then we can do something."

"Can we go to the zoo?"

"Yes. You and these animals." Ken ate and had a beer while looking at another game.

Trina put the pillow on his side and lay down watching the game with him. Ken played in her hair like old times. Little things like this she loved that from him and missed him doing it. Trina felled asleep as Ken held her. He even got up to rock their son a couple times.

Ken opened Trina's robe up and kissed her body. Then he opened her legs and began to lick and kiss her inner thigh.

Trina said, "Ken, what are you doing?"

"Shh…"

"No, Ken. I'm not ready to have sex yet."

"Okay."

He ate her out nice and slow; but before she got to cum, he stopped, got up, and took a shower. Ken stood in the middle of the floor naked and looked at Trina as she held the covers back. He smiled and climbed on the bed. Ken called the office to let them know he'd be running a little late this morning and then hung up.

Trina said, "Ken, I love you so much."

"I know you do, and I love you more. I'm so sorry, Trina." He made love to Trina, and the make-up sex was worth the wait.

Trina cried, holding on to Ken as he kissed her wet face.

"I'm here, Trina. I promise I will never hurt you again," he cried while holding her close. "Catrina Brown, I love you more than my own life. I have a sex addiction and need to get it under control."

"Yes, Ken, you do."

"Baby, there's not a day I don't want sex. Can you handle that? I mean can you lay here and tell me doing it two or three times a day, you're willing to take care of me?"

"Ken, it's self-control. I also love sex."

"Baby, you have dildos."

Trina had to laugh. "I'm telling you, I can do my wifely jobs in the morning and at night, but you need to control yourself in between those hours. So when a big-booty girl come at you, what will you do, Kenneth? Call your wife and hope she knows just what to say to her horny-ass husband?"

"No, baby. I need to walk away and remember what I have home. I'm calling this doctor today. I need to sit down and talk some things out." Ken looked over and saw his son moving around and sniffling that little cry for attention. Ken got up and said to him, "What's the problem?" He took him downstairs and got his bottle of milk. "Trina, I just took the last bottle out the fridge."

Trina started pumping more milk for the baby.

"You want to see if he'll take the breast," Ken asked.

"Yes, please."

"Those boobs are full, and I know they hurt."

KJ latched onto his mommy's nipple and begin to suck.

"That's right, son, make Mommy's breast huge for Daddy."

Ken got ready for work. "Hey, Trina, we really need to see what's going on with this house in Atlanta.

"Well, Greg's going down at the end of the month, and I was thinking of going down with him, if you could get off."

"Trina, I'm my own boss."

"No, I'm your boss."

"Ha ha ha, funny," he said as he began kissing her.

"Why he making all that noise?"

"It's good to him."

"Ken, your mom really should have broken your legs while you were a baby."

"Why you always talking about my legs. You like it?"

"Yes, I do," Trina said.

"Okay, son, come up for air. Trina, he has powder milk."

"I know, but I'll pump for your mom."

"Make some for the house 'cause I don't need him crying this evening."

"I will, Ken."

"Later."

"Love you."

"Ditto. Son, Daddy loves you," he said, kissing his cheek.

After Ken left for work, Trina got up and made some breakfast. Ken's friend, Mark, called the house and left a message that he was coming in town next week.

"Call me so we can meet up."

Trina went up to get KJ together and came back down to fix a few bottles. Trina took him to her parents' house. Timmy came out and got his lil' nephew.

Trina said, "Well damn, brother. Hello to you too."

"Trina, he looks just like Ken. You know what they say when a kid looks like that parent?"

"What?"

"They did all the work."

"He did that night. Hey, Mommy."

Her mom said, "What up?" as she took her grandson from Timmy.

"Is Daddy at work?"

"Yes. And he'll be here in a few. He already called to see if KJ's here yet."

"Mommy, please don't sit and hold him. We have him where he'll lay in his crib without crying. Here's a few blanket for the Pack 'n Play bed."

"Girl, your dad went out and got one."

Trina sat and breastfed the baby. Soon as her father walked in.

Her father asked, "Why you got that nasty tit in my grandson's mouth?"

"Daddy, look, you want me to feed him before leaving him here. Mommy, don't give him this bottle until two o'clock. He'll be ready to go over his other side until Ken picks him up. So I'll be back by 3:00 p.m." Then Trina said to her son, "Son, you're being very greedy today. Okay, I got to go." Then to Timmy, she said, "I need my truck cleaned. Come over tomorrow."

"You cooking?"

"Yes, Timmy."

Trina left to meet up with her homies for lunch. Trina walked in as the three were waiting for her.

"Sorry, I'm late. I had to feed KJ."

"How's he doing?"

"Fine."

They ordered lunch.

"How's everything going with you and the husband?"

"We are working on it. I can only take one day at a time."

Trina had a great time, but she had to go.

After she left, Ken called her. "Hey fathead, where you at?"

"On the way to my mom's."

"I'll meet you there."

"Okay."

Trina pulled up.

Ken pulled up as she was getting out her truck. He was dressed in his gym clothes and gave her a kiss, saying, "You want to come watch me play? Tia will be there."

"You sure?"

"Yes."

"Let me pump first."

"Take KJ to your mom's."

"No, let him stay here. She was talking about taking him to see Aunt Nancy. I told her no, he's not going house to house. Not until he gets six months. And he needs to go to the doctor's. So I told Daddy to come pass the house tomorrow evening."

They walked into the house and saw Trina's dad asleep with KJ on his chest. Trina took a picture of them.

"Trina, he laid out on Pop."

"That's you, Ken."

"I know. I did start that, and he loves to hear the heartbeat."

"Mommy, what's all that?"

The delivery man just left. It was a basket from her nana all the way from Japan.

Trina said, "How sweet. I will call her when I get home. We'll be back. I'm going to watch Ken play ball."

Ken asked, "Baby, your truck?" He drove. "What, it's clean in here?"

"Timmy's going to wash it tomorrow."

"Everything's in the garage to clean the truck with. You'll be done by five. If not, just leave and I'll get Cleo to drop me off at your mom's."

"How long will you be?"

"An hour or so."

He drove to the gym and grabbed his gym bag, going in. "Baby, you want a water?"

"No, thanks."

Trina saw Tia and all the fellas working out and had to get a peek at them.

Ken said, "Hey, baby, let's go."

Here we come. Trina saw this fine guy, built. He smiled at Trina and said, "Watch your step, Miss Lady."

Ken said, "Baby, watch your step because I don't want you to break your neck."

She burst out laughing.

"Ken, did you see his muscles?"

"Yes. I saw his muscles."

Trina and Tia sat up there, talking about their men.

Trina said, "Get him, husband," clapping as he made two points. Trina sat back for a while, and game was over. She said, "Maybe I should call Mitch and tell him another time."

"No, I got KJ, and Cleo's going to drop me off." Ken walked her outside and gave her a big kiss, saying, "Maybe I can rub that body down later tonight."

"I hear you talking, Kenneth."

"Love you, fat head." He walked back inside.

"Kenneth, that's your wife?" the dude asked.

"Yes, why?"

"She got a sister?"

"No."

"Damn! Man keep your eye on the prize."

"I'm doing that. Starting with your no good-ass, Ricky."

"Uh, now you Mr. Goody two-shoes."

They got to the court.

"Now you perfect."

"Man, fuck you." Ricky laughed.

"Hey, Ken, when you leave for Japan?"

"Why?"

"I'll make sure Trina's okay while you're away."

"Let me tell you something. If I thought you made a move on my wife, I would hunt you down and kill you."

"Kenneth, chill, I was just fucking with you. Stop getting all bent out of shape."

"Man, don't play with me like that. Cleo, let's roll. I need to go get KJ."

"I'm ready," he said.

Ken told the fellas, "See ya'll Friday at the card party."

Cleo said, "Bro, why do you let the fellas get to you?"

"Listen, Cleo, all I did to Trina, you don't think when I leave she not going to step out on me? Here I'm trying to fix my problem while I'm away, that I don't cheat. And now I need to worry about Trina on this end."

"Bro, you better load up on batteries and a lot of phone sex better be going on."

Ken looked at him as Cleo laughed out loud. "What you need to do bro is go over, get settled, and send for your family. Find a great doctor there for the both of them."

Trina went to the studio while Ken wasn't in his feelings. Trina and Mac did a few tracks. Mitch got there and listened to Trina sing a sad heartbreaking song.

He said, "Mac, you recording that?"

"Yeah, sounds nice, doesn't it?"

"Oh yeah, real nice."

Trina saw Mitch and waved, smiling at him.

Mitch said, "What's up, beautiful?"

"You." she said. "I'm coming out. Mac, that was hard having the baby. My gut hurts singing."

"You look great." He looked her up and down.

"Down boy," Trina told Mitch as they walked to sit down.

They talked, and Mitch asked Trina, "How's the baby?"

"He's good."

"That's my heart, Mitch."

"And Kenneth?"

"That's my pain in my heart and ass. Now I need to go. My breast are really heavy."

"To much information, Trina."

"Whatever!"

"They're so big," he said as he felt her boobs. "Bye, Trina. Go home." His dick had gotten hard.

Trina laughed. "Bye, Mitch," he said, giving him a hug.

He kissed her on the cheek.

Trina got home, and Ken was in the kitchen fixing some dinner.

"Hey, husband."

"Hey, Trina."

She gave him a big kiss and said, "I need to pump like right now." Trina grabbed the pump and sat at the table while she sat watching him cook. "They're full, and yes, they hurt. KJ sleep yet?"

"Yes, his greedy ass just went to sleep." Ken turned on the screen so they could see him.

"He so cute, Ken."

"Baby, can we talk about something really serious?"

"Yes."

"When I leave, will you wait for me? Or do I need to worry about my wife here with another man?" he asked.

"Ken, why would you ask me something like that?"

"Trina, I need to know? I mean, I'll be over there and you're be here, and you may get lonely. So I want you and Kenneth Jr. to come after I get settled. I will get the best doctors there for both of you."

"But we decided when he turned six months I would move to Japan."

"Trina, I can't let us be apart that long."

"Okay, if that's what you want," Trina said, "I feel much better now that my breast are not so full."

"So how was the studio?" Ken asked.

"It was nice. I had a hard time singing since my stomach's a little sore." Trina looked at him and ran upstairs and got the baby. "KJ, no, slow down. No rush for all this rolling." He loved to ball up when he was held, and Trina rubbed his butt as he laid on her chest.

"Well, I guess I need to talk to my staff. Tell Josh, he will be running things while I'm in Japan," Trina said.

"You have family there?"

"Yes."

"That's a good thing."

"We'll come back in a couple months, but when Kenneth turns two years old, we are out. We are moving to Atlanta. So let's get on the ball with this house."

"I'm going down with Greg next Thursday."

"Can you be good while I'm gone, Kenneth?"

"Yes."

"I have a doctor and some pills that I need to start in the morning."

Ken said, "Nosey boy, your mom's spoiling you and crying that everybody else is doing so. That hair, baby."

"Ken, leave his hair alone."

"You're looking like a little Chinese baby doll, Trina. Saturday, we get pictures done."

Ken phone rang, and it was Mark. "What's up Mark?" he said.

"I'll be in town in a couple days."

"Okay, where you staying?"

Trina hit Ken on his arm.

He said, "At a hotel."

"Okay, well, let me know when you get here. We can get together and go out to dinner."

"Later, bro."

"What, baby?" Ken asked.

"I don't want him staying here."

"I know that, Trina. I'm not going to do that to you again." He put the dishes in the washer and told his baby boy, "Come on, son, Mommy needs to clean Daddy's mess up."

"Kenneth!"

"I love you, Trina."

She cleaned the kitchen and washed bottles. Then Trina called her nana in Japan and told her that after Christmas, she would be coming to Japan to live for a while. Nana was so happy because her grandchild was coming to be close to her.

"Please don't say anything to Daddy yet. I haven't told him."

Trina went upstairs to tell Ken her nana was excited that she was coming there.

Ken held his wife. "It will be all right."

That next day, Trina went and talked to her parents and told them she would be going to Japan for a year but she would be back every two or three months for a week or so. They didn't really like the idea, but she's a married woman, so it wasn't much they could say.

She told her parents, "Until then, I will let KJ stay here while I work on the weekends. You can't get in your feelings when he's with the Browns, Mommy."

"Okay, Trina, I'll share him with the Browns. Trina, I hope you'll be back on his birthday."

"Yes, Mommy. Daddy, I already talked to Nana."

"I know she's happy."

"Yes, she's very happy," Trina said. "I need to go have a meeting with my staff."

Trina left the house, and they we're waiting for her. She broke the news.

"It's only for a year guys, and I'll be coming home. Josh will be running everything, and I will be checking in every day."

So Trina sat with Josh and went over everything. She had her accountant come, and every deposit or withdraw would go through Trina first. Trina's phone rang.

"Hello, Trina Brown speaking. How can I help you?"

A deep voice spoke on the other end. "I really hate that last name," he said.

Trina laughed. "Christopher?"

"Yes, it's me. How are you, Trina?"

"I'm better now that I'm talking to you."

"How's the baby?"

"He is very well."

"Send me a picture. My numbers the same."

"I'm doing it right now."

"So when you coming this way?" he asked.

"Chris, I'll be in Atlanta next Thursday."

"You have my address and number, so call me and we can go to dinner, if you can get away."

"Ken's not coming, Chris."

"Oh shit, it's on now!"

"No, I was thinking about you looking at your picture."

He looked and saw the baby picture she sent to him. Chris yelled, "Trina, he's Kenneth's twin."

"Yes, I know."

"He has your nose."

"He's going to be short, Chris."

"I know. Kenneth's chest is really poked out now."

Trina laughed. "I will call you when I arrive in Atlanta, Chris."

"Later, Trina."

Trina went home and fixed dinner, then went to pick KJ up, but Ken had already picked the baby up.

Ken called Trina and said, "Hey, fat head, we at my parents' house."

"Okay, I'll fixed dinner."

"You're so sweet, wifey." Before you go fix dinner.

"Trina, can you come down and give him some breastmilk 'cause he trying to find Mom's breast."

"I'm on my way."

Ken's mom was laughing so hard. "Kenneth, here take your son."

"Mom, he's funny at night. He'll be wearing Trina out sucking all night."

Trina pulled up, and her brother called to clean her truck. The trucks parked out front. I'll be back in a few minutes.

Getting her steps in.

Trina walked into the house and said hello to everyone.

"Hey, stinky man."

"Well, can I get some love?"

"Hello, husband," she said, kissing him. She took KJ, sat down to feed him, and got his belly full.

"Oh Lawd, he making all that noise eating." Trina pulled his little jeans off. "Look at those little feet. A hot damn mess, Mommy."

KJ was fighting the nipple.

Trina said, "It's like he's not getting enough."

Kent walked in and said, "I've seen enough vagina and boobs for one day."

Trina asked Kent, "Why is he fighting the nipple?"

"That's Ken's child."

"Well, we know that, but why?"

"Trina, is the milk coming out?"

Ken said, "Let me check?"

"Oh my Lawd," Grandma Gwen said. "He didn't just suck Trina's breast in front of us?"

"Yes, he did. It's coming out. He's just nasty, Mom."

Ken's dad came in. "Oh, Lawd, the whole crew here."

"Hello, Pop, how are you?"

"I'm doing okay, Trina."

"Dad, you look tired today."

"Had a rough day, Kenneth. I have two months left, and then I'm done with all the bullshit. I may come to Japan for a while and leave Gwen here."

"Whatever, Kenneth. Bye!" He took his grandson and went in the kitchen. "Gwen, what's for dinner?

"I thought we were going out tonight."

He stood there looking at Kent. He laughed out loud.

"We about to go home," Ken said. "I need a ride. Timmy's cleaning my truck."

They left for home, and Timmy and Mel were shining the wheels on Trina's truck.

Ken said, "Well, damn, I need my truck cleaned too."

She told her brother thanks and then paid him.

Ken said, "I need my truck done, bro."

"Ken, you keep going to the shop because you're too damn picky."

"It smells good inside, like baby powder."

Ken and Trina went inside to bath the baby, then they had a quiet dinner.

He said, "Let's go, little mama," and he went up and ran a bath so they could relax in it.

Trina took good care of her man that night and went to sleep happy.

That next week Trina was going to Atlanta with Greg. Ken had Mark coming while Trina was out of town. What Ken or Trina didn't know was that Zena was also coming along.

Ken dropped Greg and Trina off at the airport.

"Ken, Mommy will have KJ tonight. So when you get off, please go get him."

"Baby, I got our son. Don't worry. Just call me when you get there."

"I will. Try to stay out of trouble."

"I will."

Trina got on the plane.

Greg said, "I have a few things to take care of tonight, but I will be back in the morning so we can go check on the house."

"Sounds good."

Going to the hotel, Greg took an overnight bag.

Trina called Kenneth.

"What's up, fat head?"

"Nothing. About to go for a long swim, then go get some dinner. I'm a little tired today."

"Well, I'm going out with the fellas and then get back home."

"Call me in the morning."

"I will."

"I love you."

"Love you more."

A knock came on the hotel room door. It was Chris looking sexy as ever. He came in, giving her a hug.

"Girl, you looking thick."

Trina said. "You swimming?"

"Yes."

He changed, and so did Trina.

"I'm glad to see your hair's long again."

"Yes, I like it at the neck. Stop looking at me like that, Chris."

"I'm just glad we became friends again."

"Yes, me too."

"Let's go swim."

They walked down to the pool. They then sat, talking, and did a few laps, until Trina had to pump again.

"How about we just order in and talk some more."

"Okay."

So Trina ordered the food and some wine from room service. Trina opened up to Chris, and he was a little upset about everything she was telling him.

"You're going to Japan for what eight or nine months?" he asked.

"Yes, I'll be home quite a bit though."

"Please stay in touch with me."

After sitting and having a wonderful dinner together, Ken was in the shower and Mark left out to go see his mom, leaving Zena there. She had her tubes tied after another miscarriage. Ken got out of the shower to find Zena laying on his bed.

He told her, "Zena, you need to roll out. Hey, Mark!"

"Oh, he left out, Kenneth."

"Well, you need to get off my bed, like now!"

She got up, took her hands, and started rubbing on Ken's dick.

"Zena, stop, please."

She dropped down and began to suck his dick.

"Uh, shit. You suck dick so damn good." Then he moved her, leaning her over the chair and fuck the hell out of her ass. Ken pulled Zena up and said, "Open your mouth," as he nutted down her throat, and she choked.

After he finished, he said to her, "Now get out my room, and don't you ever try this shit again."

Ken called Mark.

"What wrong, bro?"

"Man, come get your bitch out my house." Then he hung up.

Ken went downstairs after he got dressed. Cleo got there.

"So, Ken, why Zena sitting outside?"

"I put her outside. This bitch want to play games I don't have time for, Cleo."

Mark pulled up.

"Mark, did you put your girl up to some bullshit after I told you what me and Trina was going through?"

"No. Zena, what you do?"

"Nothing."

"Bro, I love you, and you know how we get down together. Not alone," Mark said.

"Hey, your girl dropped down and handled business. Had me bang that ass. Check her."

"Get in the car, Zena."

"Bro, I love you too, but I'm trying to save my marriage."

Trina and Chris stood on the patio, and he said, "Trina, I miss you so much."

Trina said, "I need a drink," walking inside.

Chris kissed Trina. He came out of his robe, and so did Trina.

He said, "Trina, rubbers?"

And she said, "On the nightstand."

Chris asked her, "Why you so nervous? It's not like we never did it before," as he began kissing and sucking on Trina's nipples. He opened Trina legs and eased it inside, and she moaned out so loud. It had been a long time since they had sex. They had wild sex together, and he whispered in her ear, "I need you to cum as I bang you hard. Trina, cum for me."

She held on to him with her nails in his skin, leaving scratches all on his back. She said, "I'm cummin, Chris." Trina got hers, and she keep going until he couldn't anymore.

He laid there and told her, "That's how we do it," and kissed her.

"Catrina, I know you have a family, but remember this, if you ever need me, just to talk or a place to get away, I'm here for you."

"Thank you."

"Now, can you please put some ice on my back? Those nails. I still have marks on my back from our last time together."

"I'm sorry."

Trina cleaned his back, and she put ice on it, which felt really good.

"I hope Val don't come in town for a couple weeks."

"Trina, I want you to promise me something."

"What's that?"

"If you and Kenneth don't make it, you'll give us a try?"

"I would. But I'm not thinking like that."

He lay with Trina until 5:00 a.m. After making love to her one last before leaving, he went home to get ready for work.

Trina took a shower and straightened the bed up.

Greg came in around 7:30 a.m.

"Why I smell body oil?"

Trina told him that Chris came by.

"Trina!"

"Hush, Greg. Let's go have breakfast, and see what's going on at the house."

Trina had a busy morning after their breakfast. She met with the contractors and introduced them to Greg.

"You will talk to Greg and my dad a lot when I leave the States and until I get back." Trina looked at the plans and said, "I want trees coming up my long road. The gate at the road and the fence will go all around the house. I don't care. Let's get this done. My house will be done in six months?"

"Yes, Mrs. Brown."

"You deal with me. This is my house, so whatever Mr. Brown told you, erase it from your brain. I'm the deed owner of this house and land. You call me and only me, until I let you know that I'm leaving the States. Got it?"

"Yes, ma'am."

Greg looked around. "Thank you." Greg said. "Trina, you serious?"

"Listen, Greg, my grandfather left me all this land, and I won't let Ken screw with it, like he screw his whores."

"Okay then."

"Now, let's go shopping so I can get back to my baby tomorrow. Greg, you drive while I pump."

"Oh, Lawd!"

Trina called to check on KJ, and her mom said, "Ken got off early and came and got the baby. He said they was hitting the mall before going home."

"Go ahead, Mr. Kenneth."

She called Ken, and he was in the mall.

"Hey, baby, we miss you."

"How much you miss me?"

"Enough for me to say hurry home. I held your pillow last night."

"Aw, Ken, I'll be home tomorrow."

"Okay, I'll be to pick you up at 2:30 p.m."

"Thank you."

"I'm picking our pictures up now. Trina, they really look nice."

"I can't wait to see them. I'll call you later. I'm pumping, and Greg's driving."

"Later."

"Love you both. Kiss my little man for me." Trina hung up.

Greg and Trina shopped, had an early dinner, went back to their rooms, and relaxed that night.

When Trina arrived back home, Ken was standing there waiting for her with their son.

Greg said, "Look at wiggles all dressed up. Where y'all been?"

"A birthday party at Cleo's. We didn't stay long since the kids was all in his face. I told Cleo we had to go." Ken's beeper went off once, but it wasn't anything important. "I went to the doctor's office, and they removed it. That's good right?"

"Yes, baby, very good."

Greg put KJ in his seat and played with him. Ken took Greg home, and then they went over his parents' house to give a few of their pictures to everybody. They made their rounds, giving out pictures, so they could go home.

Ken and Trina were packing because they had a few weeks left in the house. So they decided to put everything in storage and stay with Trina's parents until the left to go overseas.

Trina said, "I need to go get my shot before I leave the States. I was supposed to have gotten it a few days ago." Trina's been using the foam sponge before having sex.

Ken said, "Baby, come to bed."

"Ken, I need to go in the bathroom."

"For what?"

"I need to put this foam sponge up inside me."

"Come here."

"What, husband?"

He pulled her down on top of him and said, "Kiss me."

So she did.

He told Trina, "I'm feeling real horny."

"Ken, that's nothing new to me. Let me go take care of everything."

"Why?"

"Because we have junior already."

Ken acted like a little kid.

Trina got up and went in the bathroom and inserted the foam sponge inside of her. She got back in bed. "Let's give it thirty minutes, and then we can do this."

"Fuck that." He got on Trina and said, "Let's make love," kissing her body all over.

"Ken, KJ's only six months."

"You love me, right?"

"Yes."

"Then let make KJ a lil' brother or sister. Please, baby."

So she gave in that night.

"You know moving in with your parents, I need to get all I can now."

"Good night, Ken."

Trina woke up to feed the baby. "This your last breastfeeding, so get all you can."

"Baby, you all right?"

"Yes, go back to sleep."

"What you looking at, Kenneth?"

"Hurry up and get Kenneth Jr. back to sleep, so I can lay on my pillow."

Trina rocked the baby back to sleep and got back in bed. Ken was all over her. Trina lay on her stomach, and Ken said, "I'll ride that ass."

He was on Trina that whole week. It wasn't no better when they moved in with her parents.

He asked Trina to come have lunch with him at his office. He had a nice lunch set up.

"So one week, you ready?"

"Yes and no. I haven't come on yet."

"Really, baby?"

"I'm going over there and having a baby."

"So when you come back, you'll have another one surprise." Ken smiled. He got up, locking his door. He said, "Simms, I'm out to lunch."

"Yes, sir."

Ken asked Trina to come to him, and he put his hands up her dress and pulled her panties off. He took his clothes off.

Trina asked, "How many times you've done this?"

"None."

She sat on top of him and started riding. Ken picked her up and stood with her back up against the wall, and they got down. She experienced things with Ken that she had never done before with him, making out in his office, and even in the fitting room at the store.

Trina said, "Husband, I need to go get our son from your mom."

He slapped her on the ass.

They went in the bathroom to freshen up. Trina thanked her husband for lunch.

"Wait until we get to Japan."

Christmas Eve, Trina was not feeling good. Ken decided they would call it an early night. Trina was not telling him that she was a month pregnant as she lay on Ken's chest, sick.

"You want some crackers?"

"Yes, please."

He went downstairs and grabbed the crackers and a ginger ale soda. He went back to the room. "Baby, here eat the crackers."

"Thanks.'

After the holidays, Ken, Trina, and KJ were off to Japan. It was a sad day for all their families and friends at the airport.

Ken told his wife, "We'll be back in a couple months, stop crying." Kenneth looked at Trina. "We have a beautiful house there, a nanny and housekeeper. What more can we ask for? And your nana lives two miles away."

It seemed like forever getting there, but finally, they arrived with a driver waiting on them.

"Welcome, Mr. Brown and Mrs. Brown."

"Thank you. Home, please."

"I haven't been here in so long. I forgot how pretty it was. KJ, we're home, son."

Trina had a big smile on her face, seeing the house Ken had bought as their home away from home.

Ken's truck was out front. Trina had left her truck with her parents.

Walking inside, Trina said, "It's beautiful, Ken. Look at the wood floors. I got to put these floors in the house back home." She took a picture to send the designer remodeling their house back in the states. Trina posted a picture of the house and said, "We're here and our new life has begun."

"Trina, come look out back."

"Oh, Ken, it's a monkey."

"Now you see why we have the screened-in deck."

"But they're so cute," she said.

Ken told Trina, "Do not bring no animals in the house! Okay. And don't feed them. I mean it, Trina."

"Okay, damn!"

"I know you, Trina."

"Can we get a kitten, Kenneth?"

"Hell no!"

"A dog?"

"No! If you get lonely, play with KJ." He laughed while looking at him crawling around on the floor.

The little man was starting to get into everything, but when he heard his father's voice and the word *no*, he listened. KJ always went to Mommy. Trina got his walker out and let him explore around the house while Ken put up the baby gates.

KJ was looking at his dad, and Ken told him, "Yes, for your bad ass."

KJ smiled, rolling around in his walker. "This kid's moving too fast."

"Ken, who's that coming in the house?"

The lady was dressed in black-and-white outfit.

"That's Sukie, our housekeeper," Ken said. "Mrs. Suki." Kenneth hugged her. "Trina, this lady will come in every morning to clean and help you with anything you need."

Trina smiled as she hugged Suki.

"Trina, when I was here taking my business classes of my last year in school, I met her and she's been like a second mother to me ever since. She is the best. I trust Suki with Kenneth."

"All right, I'm with that, husband. Ken, we don't have a pool?"

"Come on, Suki. You have Kenneth for a few."

"Yes," she said, "Come, little one."

Ken took Trina by the hand as they walked downstairs to the basement. It was like another world with a huge indoor pool inside a cave.

Trina screamed, "Oh my God, I'm in heaven. Ken, this house…!"

"I knew when I saw it that I had to buy it. Look, we may only be here until the end of the year, but it's a wonderful getaway."

"Ken, I want this in Atlanta."

"Trina, you know how much this would cost? We don't have a basement in that house. That was the reason you added a clubhouse, remember?"

"I know that. But, Kenneth, can't we have a cave made onto that house?"

"Trina, that's a lot of money, and who would be designing this?

"I will just send a picture to Scott and Neal."

"Trina, you have a budget for this house. Now I know my money's now your money, but we need to save for rainy days and our kid's education."

"Ken, I know all this. That's why I'm paying for this myself."

"You the boss, handle it. Remember, you want this and you will maintain the pool."

"Can we come down here tonight?"

"Yes, for a little while. I start work tomorrow with a new staff and lots to do."

"You will be fine."

"Hell, I know that, but will they be fine?" Then he took Trina upstairs to see the bedrooms.

She said, "Nice, Ken. It's really nice. Now if this bed isn't big enough for us three, I don't know what to say or do. I pray this baby won't be a rough sleeper like you, Kenneth. I guess you just lay in one spot all night, huh?"

"Sure do. Protecting my dick that keeps getting kicked all night long."

Trina laughed, saying, "Ken, stop lying. Where's KJ's crib at?"

"It's in his room."

"My baby is not sleeping alone yet."

Trina looked at our son's room. It was huge, a room to die for.

Ken said, "He's sleeping in this room tonight. Two months ago you took the titty away, and now he's staying in this room. Mommy and Daddy need to do them before this little one comes out the oven."

Trina walked out the room and went downstairs where KJ was sitting in his chair eating rice with chicken, and she choked up.

Trina said, "That smells good."

Sue was the cook, and she cooked Japanese dishes for them.

Trina said, "Thank you, Sue."

Then Ken said, "Baby, I know you're going to cook, right?"

"I might."

He was smiling and sat down to a plate of food. Ken was talking shit.

"This some bullshit here."

"Kenneth, you right at home eating rice."

His son wanted to share his food with him, but Ken said, "No, thank you, son. You eat it all up."

Ken called home, and it was nighttime back there.

"Dad, what you doing?"

"Been waiting for you to call me."

"Sorry, Dad, Trina in here going crazy over the pool and our cook fixed her favorite dishes."

"Where's my grandson?"

"He's eating. What else?"

"Kenneth, please tell me he's eating something other than rice."

Ken said, "Rice and chicken."

"Should have known."

"Hey, Pop, love you."

"Tell Trina I miss and love her also."

"She hear you. Pop you need to come here soon."

"I'll be out there soon."

"Dad, are you serious?"

"Yes, I told you I'll be there. I'm working something out."

"Dad, don't worry about money. I set you an account up for anything you'll need. And so did Trina with her parents."

"I know, son. I will let you know when I'm coming. Give little KJ a big kiss for me."

"I love you all, Dad. We'll talk tomorrow."

Trina called her mom, and it was a very emotional conversation with the two of them. Trina's no longer close to home, and her mom knows Trina has her health problems, and it would be hard to get to her mom.

"I'm okay. Please don't be sad. I'll call you every day, and I'll video chat with you. So tonight before I go to bed, I'll call you again. It will be morning there, so get Timmy to hook the laptop up for you."

"Okay."

"Mommy, when I come home, you need to come back with me. Mommy you will love it here."

Ken looked at Trina and knew she would have a hard time living in Japan with her parents and brother thousands of miles away.

"Baby, won't you go lie down and get some rest for a little while. I got KJ."

Trina walked away.

"Hey, Trina, you will be okay. It takes time."

Kenneth sat back with his son, relaxing, until they both fell asleep down on the sofa.

The nanny took his son up to his room and laid him in the crib.

Ken woke up. Not feeling his son on his chest, he began to panic.

Mrs. Suki said, "Kenneth, calm down. He's in his crib. You was sleeping so good that I took him up to his room. Gee wiz, son, get a grip."

"I know, Mrs. Suki, we're just so used to being with our baby."

"Well, I'm here, so you and Trina can get out and focus on this marriage you been telling me about."

"Yes, ma'am."

"Kenneth, you need control this sex problem while you're here. There are too many woman looking for men like yourself with money."

"Mrs. Suki, Trina has the money, not me."

"Smart girl."

"What! You supposed to be on my side."

"Not this time. I'll kick your bowlegged ass if you fuck up again. I'm not your dad to clean up your mess when you fuck up." Mrs. Suki always told it like it was. "Kenneth, you know me, I don't sugarcoat nothing. You have known me for a long time, and I'm not going to change. You have a wonderful wife that I've seen in this short time. Whatever happened to that funny-looking girl?"

"Who?"

"Nikki, that's her name."

"Oh, her crazy ass back home trying to still piss Trina off. Trina wants to whip that butt so bad." He was smiling.

"She's gonna whip your ass before it's over with if you keep on playing dumb. Stop thinking with your dick, Kenneth."

"Yes, ma'am. You done preaching, Mother Suki?"

"For now, until you act up. Then I'm going to preach again and again until I soften that brick head of yours."

Ken went upstairs and lay down beside Trina, just watching her sleep. He heard his son whining as he woke up. Ken went over to see what his son was fussing for. He picked KJ up and said, "Oh no! No nipple when you with me."

The baby made a face at his father.

"Let's get changed and go for a stroll while Mommy sleep."

He said, "Da, da."

"Yes, Daddy!" Ken changed KJ and took him downstairs to Suki mother dearest.

"We going out for a stroll," he told her. Ken got out the baby stroller, then they headed out strolling the neighborhood.

When Trina woke up, she called Ken.

"Yes, dear," he answered the phone.

"Hey, it's time for you and KJ to come back so he can take his meds."

"Yes, ma'am, we're on our way."

Trina was down in the kitchen and had the cook fix an Asian dish while she baked and fried some fish and made cornbread too. Trina sat with the cook, and they came up with a menu for the week.

Trina said, "Tomorrow, we will go to the market."

Sue said, "I will be here in the morning. Mr. Brown, what you would like for breakfast?"

"Something good, please."

She knew his favorites in the morning: two waffles, a hard-boiled egg, two slices of bacon, and oatmeal with brown sugar.

Ken said, "Let her know, baby."

"Ken, give your son his medicine, please."

Trina called her nana's phone and said, "Papa, it's Trina. I'm here in Japan."

He was so happy to hear she was in Japan that he yelled, letting everyone know that she was there.

"I'll be over to see everyone tomorrow. Please tell nana when she comes back, okay, Papa?" Trina said. Then Trina sang in Ken's face, "I'm going to see my grandparents tomorrow."

"Baby, you finish cooking?"

"Yes."

He pointed upstairs.

"Later, Kenneth."

"Damn! Who can I call this time of morning?"

"Ken, don't you dare call anybody until around nine or ten tonight."

"Around that time I'll be banging your back out, and I won't need to call anyone."

The staff laughed at Ken.

Trina said, "Son, let's eat."

Trina fixed KJ some baby food.

"Why he get so excited when he sees that nasty-looking food?"

"The same way your ass get excited seeing nasty hoes," Trina told him.

Mrs. Suki burst out laughing. "Kenneth, I like her."

Ken got mad and took his plate and went out back.

Trina sat down and ate while Mrs. Suki gave the baby his dinner.

Ken asked, "My son finish eating yet?"

"Yes, he is."

So Ken took him and went upstairs, grabbing his bottle as he left the kitchen.

"Ken?"

"Trina, not now, please."

He bathed his son, gave him a bottle, and rocked him to sleep. Ken put KJ in his room.

Trina asked, "Where you going?"

"To find some hoes," he said, walking downstairs with his towel.

Trina went and checked on KJ.

Ken got his speakerphone and walked downstairs to say good night to the staff.

Trina locked the door and went in the basement where Ken was swimming in the pool. She took her clothes off, dressed in just her bra and panties.

"Ken, I'm sorry if I said something to offend you."

"Look, Trina, I know I cheated. Don't keep throwing it up in my face." He was pissed. "We went from baby food to a hoe. Really, Trina! Don't bring that vibe here 'cause we left that shit back home."

Shee apologized as she stood in front of him and put her hands around him, kissing on his chest. Then she bit his nipple. "What can I do to make you feel better?"

"I can name a few things," he said.

Trina gave him some head action as he held on to the rail.

He yelled out, "Ooh, baby…please don't stop." It got so good to him that he pulled Trina's bra off and pulled her up, laying her on the diving board to make love. Their make-up sex was the best love-making they shared together. Both were so worn-out after that workout, the only thing they could do was make it upstairs, check on their son, and hit the bed, holding each other that night.

In the morning, Ken got up, putting KJ in bed with Trina and let them sleep while he went down and enjoyed his breakfast. He asked Sue to find some mint cookies and ice cream while she's out at the market today.

"Yes, sir, anything else?

"No, that's it. Thanks." Kenneth sat, reading the paper. "Mama Suki, I'm glad we can read this damn paper."

"I'm glad also."

He heard Trina moving around. She came down looking rough.

"Morning sickness?"

"Yes."

"Breakfast, Mrs. Brown?"

"No, thank you."

"Baby, you need to eat."

"I will. Not just now, Kenneth.

"Mrs. Suki, can you please feed KJ."

"Giggles," Ken said to his son.

Mrs. Suki started talking in Japanese to him.

"Oh, Lawd, Mama Suki, don't start that with him. It's bad enough Trina does it."

Trina sat in the living room logging online to Skype with her mom.

Timmy answered, "What's up, sis?"

They both smiled and started talking.

"You seen Nana yet?"

"No, not yet, but I miss you, brother."

"Dittos."

"Where's Mommy?"

He yelled for their mother and father.

Trina saw her mom's face.

"Oh, Lawd, Trina you look terrible."

"I know. I'll get it together in a few. Mrs. Suki, is KJ still eating?"

Ken said, "No, greedy didn't want that mess. Sue's fixing him some egg whites now.

"Okay, KJ, look there's Nana," Trina's mom said. "Look at my baby. Uh, Trina, I miss him. I need to come there."

"I can't do this, Ken."

"Mom, you want to come out for a few weeks?"

"Yes."

"Daddy coming?"

"Billy, can you get off?" she asked her husband.

"Lena, bills needs to get paid here."

Ken said, "Baby, work it out. I need to go."

"All right, have a great day."

"I'll call you later."

"Remember, you're not back home, so don't be cursing people out."

"I won't. Tell Nana hello, and I'll see her soon."

"I will, Kenneth."

"Bye." She kissed him goodbye.

Ken had a driver for work so that Trina could have the truck at home during the day.

"Mommy, when you want to come?"

"Book my flight."

"Daddy, please come out with Mommy. I will pay the bills Mommy have on her card, if anything needs to be paid."

"I didn't know all that."

"Oops!"

"You and your mom be doing some sneaky shit."

They all laughed.

"I'll come out for two weeks."

"Really, Daddy?"

"Yes, your mom can stay longer. Hell, she can stay until you come back."

"I just might do that."

"Mommy, you will love this house."

"Hey, Timmy, you want to come out too?"

"Hell, no, I'm good. Send me a postcard. Hey, sis, do something with my nephew's hair. He'll fit in here with a ponytail."

"Yes, he will. Okay, Mommy, I'm going to hang up and book the flights. I'll email everything to you."

Trina booked her parents flights for Wednesday evening and sent everything to them. Trina went back upstairs and got KJ dressed, then gave him to his nanny.

"Mrs. Suki, he's bad, isn't he?"

"No, not at all."

Trina sat down and ate some toast and drank some tea. "Sue, I'll be ready in a few."

Then Trina went up to make her bed. She found herself putting on her bigger-size jeans and a top since her hips were wider and her boobs had gotten bigger. No one knew she was pregnant though. Trina took her hair down and went down to get her purse. She crept out the house so that KJ wouldn't see her. Mrs. Suki kept him busy until she made it out the house.

"Sue, you can drive."

"Yes, ma'am."

"And, Sue, please call me Trina."

"Yes, ma'am," she said, smiling.

"Okay, so where's the store? The market's our first stop to get all the meats you want. I will need lots of meats since my parents are coming to visit."

They brought all types of food and vegetables. Then to the grocery store for Mr. Brown's mint cookies and ice cream. Trina loaded up on junk food. Trina got KJ some of his favorite baby cookies.

She said, "I guess I better get some fruit, Sue."

Finally, they were finished, and Trina said, "Okay, let's go home. I need to go to my nana's house. I like the shopping here."

They left the store and went back to the house, and KJ was being nosey and into everything.

Trina said, "KJ, what you doing?"

He was looking in the bags again when Trina's phone rang. It was Ken calling her.

"Husband, why you didn't call my phone?"

"I did."

Trina looked. "My bad. It was turned down. How's everything?"

"Okay. I have one brother here in my whole building, and he's a snitching ass, baby. He has told on everyone on this floor, and it's not even lunchtime yet."

Trina laughed out loud. "Well, good thing you're the damn boss because you would probably be fired."

"You telling me?"

"Yes."

"Now you ready to tell them you pregnant?"

"Umm, no. And don't you tell them either, Ken."

"I won't." He laughed. "Baby, "I need to go."

"Later, smart ass."

"Later, baby."

"Mrs. Suki, we out. Sue, the spaghetti, salad, and French bread, have it ready around 4:30 p.m. I will be back around the time my husband arrives home."

Trina packed up and left, driving to her nana's.

Blowing the horn as she got out the car. Her grandfather came outside. He was the coolest sixty-five-year-old granddad.

"Papa," she said, kissing him.

"Trina, look at you."

KJ was looking like, "Who is this?"

Trina gave him the bag, and she got KJ to look at his great-grandpa.

"Trina, he's handsome."

"KJ, see Papa?"

He lay on Trina's chest, holding on tight to her top.

They walked in, and Nana was waiting. She hugged and kissed her granddaughter.

"Look at KJ."

His great-grandma kissed him and took him in her arms.

"Nana, he's spoiled."

"I know. Your father told me."

"Guess what? Mommy and Daddy are coming on Thursday. They leaving next Wednesday night."

"Oh my goodness. You miss them, don't you?"

"Yes. I'm about to get my mother to stay with me.

"Really, Trina, really?!"

"Oh yeah, or I'm going back home."

"Trina, you need to do something to keep yourself busy. Work on your line. Put your shoes in the stores over here. I mean, not your high prices, but at a little cheaper cost."

"I may do that."

"Or start a website while I'm here."

"Nana, you may be onto something."

Trina had lunch and lay down with KJ.

Her grandpa said, "So Trina, when you have this other baby?"

"Sir?"

"You heard me."

Trina told him, "August, but please don't say nothing…I haven't told anyone yet."

"Trina, you can see it. Your nose gotten bigger."

"Oh, Papa, stop it. And, Nana, my papa sure looking good lately. What you doing to him?"

"With his fine self."

He laughed.

"Papa, Daddy looks so much like you.

"You think so?" he asked.

"Yes."

She took pictures with her grandparents and with KJ when he woke up. Trina posted on her page and let everyone see her other side of the family and where she gets her beauty from.

Trina bust out laughing and told her grandpa, "Christine said you're looking real sexy, Papa."

He started cheesing hard. Nana wasn't paying him no mind at all.

Trina's cousins and one aunt that lived there came to the house. She and Trina were four years apart. Her aunt calls Trina a spoiled brat.

"She's a big hater," Trina told her grandparents.

They just don't get along.

"It's time to go…my husbands about to get off work."

"Hey, niece."

"Hey, Wanda, this KJ."

"Yes, hello, looking like your ole crazy-looking daddy."

"I'll make sure to tell him that when I get home."

Ken couldn't stand her either.

"Trina, what y'all renting that house?"

"No, it's ours. We'll be using it when we need to come back and forth or just to vacation, or when Mommy and Daddy want to come visit her sisters and other brother."

"So I can stay in your house when you go back home to the states?"

"Hell, no. Papa and Nana, I'm out."

Trina's cousins Tye and Boogie said, "Tee, we'll be over later so we can get started on your website."

"Okay, come for dinner at 5:00 p.m. sharp."

"Be there in a few." She left and went home.

Trina stripped KJ down to his Pampers, socks, and undershirt. When Ken came home looking at his truck, she said, "I see you looking at your truck."

"What's up, baby?"

"Kenneth, what you got in your hair?"

KJ was happy to see his father.

"Trina, what you do to his hair?"

"Nothing."

"You know what I'm talking about." He took KJ's hair out the ponytail. "Can you just put three braids?"

Trina braided his hair so Ken wouldn't be tight all day.

Ken asked, "We having guest?" while looking in the pot.

"My cousins coming over. They're going to help me with my website here."

"What you ready to do, baby?"

"Well, so I won't be homesick, I thought I would do my shoe line here. Open up a little store, and see how it goes."

"Go for it." He slapped her ass. "I'm going to wash up and get out these clothes."

Trina sat at the piano and sang while dinner was being warmed. KJ sat quietly by, listening to her.

Her cousins came over and told her, "Cuz, you still got it." They stood there listening to Trina sing to KJ.

Ken came back down. "What going on?"

"She's singing to Kenneth."

"Yeah, he's enjoying it very much," Boogie said to Ken.

Trina played the music on the piano, and KJ was clapping his little hands. Ken hated that song she always sing. It sounded like she was packing her suitcase and telling him bye. Trina smiled at KJ waving bye-bye to his daddy, Ken.

"Trina, you teaching my son some shady shit, I see."

"Come on, Ken, sing for KJ so we can eat."

"Okay, come on."

They sat down, and Trina sang with Kenneth.

Mrs. Suki came out listening while Tye was recording them.

They hugged, and then Ken said, "That's it, let's eat."

"KJ, you heard Daddy."

He went rolling down the hallway.

Ken called "Kenneth! Come on eat. Let's go!"

He went straight to his father, and Ken picked him up. KJ was trying to give Ken a kiss.

"Close your mouth and stop sucking up like your mother."

"Suck up?" Trina said. "Whatever, Ken."

Tye and Boogie's were both in the bathroom around the corner. They both came out asking Trina if they all got a cook.

"Yes, I'm sorry. Mrs. Suki, these my cousins, Boogie and Tye. And this is Sue, our cook."

"Well, hello," said the guys.

"Hello and welcome," she replied. "Mr. Brown, anything else you need for tonight?"

"No, we good, Sue."

"Tomorrow I'll be going in around 8:00 a.m. Can I have this for lunch tomorrow?"

"Yes, sir."

"Trina, don't fix me no damn rice this week. They welcome me with lunch. Trina, we had rice and chicken. So please, I'll eat noodles, no rice. Fuck, I just left back home, and you are killing me with rice."

Tye said, "Yo, Trina, you still eat rice like that?"

"Yes, our this kid see it and get happy like his nana when she get out of church," Trina rolled. "I'm telling Lena on your ass."

They finished eating.

Trina sat at the computer to put together a website and open her shoe line up to Japan.

"So, cousin, I can take you to a spot near the business where everyone will pass the shop."

"Okay, tomorrow at 10:00 a.m."

"Okay, I'll call my girl. She rents the spaces, and she can meet us."

After they left, Ken was sitting on the bed reading reports.

Trina said, "My stink gone to sleep?"

"Yes, Trina. He's a handful at bedtime."

Trina said, "So what you reading?"

"Nothing, baby. You wouldn't understand."

"Oh wow! I understand the business back home but not here?" she asked him.

"Baby, I didn't mean it like that." His phone went off. It was Simms, his assistant back home. He looked at the text and texted back.

Trina said, "Wow!" So she waited and didn't say a word.

When he went in the bathroom to take his shower, she got his cell phone and he had a pass code on it. Trina figured it out and was reading all the text message from Ms. Simms. "That bitch."

"Kenny, my lease is almost up, need you to renew, and send the information."

Trina sent everything to her cell phone. As the water turned off, Trina eased her message, turned his phone light off, and sat it back down.

That night Trina went to sleep. And that morning, she got up and went downstairs and she hooked Ken's ass right up, putting laxative in his tea.

Trina called Mitch up and said, "I'll be home in two weeks. I need to sit down and go over some paperwork with you."

"What's going on?"

"I'll explain it when I see you, but just say, I had enough, and I'm about check his ass."

"Oh shit! Okay, see you in two weeks."

She got off the phone to handle business at home and then waited for her cousin to come pick her up.

Ken sat down, asking Trina, "What's wrong?"

"Nothing, husband, everything just lovely. Don't you worry your sexy self about anything. Mama got this all under control. You just sit and eat your breakfast all up like a nice husband." Trina then gave him a kiss.

"Mrs. Suki, I need to go now."

"Ken, you okay with the menu tonight?"

"Yes, sounds good."

"See you later on."

"All right, baby."

Trina kissed her son and left the house.

Ken looked at Mama Suki and asked, "What's up with Trina this morning?"

"I have no idea. What you do?"

"Nothing at all."

"Ummm," she said. "Boy, you better be crossing all your t's and dotting all i's because Mrs. Brown seem she can be something else if you piss her off."

"No, we okay, Mama Suki."

"Okay, just letting you know."

"Look, she got her parents coming to keep her company."

Trina went to look at the space, and it was amazing. So she decided to go for it and closed the deal. She went to lunch with and her cousins and made all her phone calls to have everything moving along quickly to open a little store. Trina's cousins wanted to help her since they knew sales really well. Now they were a team.

Trina said, "When I leave, I want you two running everything, not your hungry-ass mother. Deal?"

"Trina, it's a deal," they said.

"I will come here every few months to check on thing. I may go home before I have my baby. Like in June or July."

She gave them a fair price to run the store there in Japan, and they was very pleased with her offer.

Trina went home.

While Trina was in the kitchen, she heard the front door open, and it was Ken.

Trina said, "What you doing home?"

"My stomach not so well."

"You want something."

"Yes, we have ginger ale?"

"Yes, I'll bring you some upstairs."

Trina got the laxative and poured half in the glass and the rest was soda. She looked at Sue and said, "Shhh!"

Sue laughed so hard at her.

Trina went upstairs and told her husband, "Here you go. Take a nap, and I'll call you when dinner's fixed."

"Thank you. How did everything go?"

"Great." She walked out.

Trina decided not to involve Ken in any of her business from that point on. She went down in the office and made a call.

"Yes, this is Mrs. Brown. The rental that my husband has in his name, I'm the overseer of all the accounts, and we no longer need this rental. So Ms. Simm's needs to vacate as soon as possible. We will send her a notice. Thank you so much."

Now Trina called the banks and had all accounts put on an alert. No more than two hundred dollars a day could be withdrawn from Ken's accounts at home and in Japan. She had to be notified if any large withdraws would occur. Ken messed up when he gave Trina access to all his accounts. She was now the account holder. He changed everything before leaving the States since the Feds was on his back.

Trina sat reading a book to KJ, as she did every chance she could. He was a quick learner for an eight-month-old. Trina called Chris, and he was surprised to hear from her.

"Chris, is this a bad time?"

"No, not at all. How you been?"

"Good. And you?"

"Great, since I heard your voice."

"So I'll be home in two weeks."

"Really?"

"Yes. I'm glad."

"I'll be at my mom's house."

"I hope to see you, Trina."

"You will."

KJ was grabbing the phone, saying, "Da, da, da."

"No, it's not Daddy."

Chris laughed. "So you having another baby?"

"Yes, you were shocked when I text and told you?"

"Yes, very much. So when can I get my child? That's all I want."

"Chris, bye!

"Trina, wait. I love you and always will."

"Later, Chris."

Then Ken came down and tried to eat but couldn't. He was in the bathroom all night. Trina smiled, then went to sleep.

Ken couldn't make it to work that next day. She was hooking him up. When her parent got there, Trina sat up that whole night talking to her mom.

"Trina, what have you done to Ken?"

"Nothing, just making him suffer a little right now."

"Girl, you learned all my tricks, didn't you?"

"Sure did."

They laughed.

Her father came down, yelling, "Trina! Stop doing what you doing to Kenneth."

"What you talking about? Oh, you know?"

"Stop giving him laxative,"

Trina said, "He want to fuck around. This is what fucking around does for you. Sorry, Daddy, but I'm mad."

"Well, stop it."

Trina went upstairs to give Ken some power drink.

"Here, drink it. Ken, don't fuck with me. I'm the last woman you want to fuck with right now. I'll leave you high and dry."

"Trina, you're an evil bitch!!"

"I been called worse things. And by the way, your bitch has twenty-six days to get out that rental. I'm being nice."

He looked but couldn't say anything to Trina.

She went down and washed some clothes.

When Ken came back down, Trina told him she'll be going back home to take care of some business. "Just to let you know, I'll be gone about two weeks."

"Your trip to Boston is in June."

"I won't be able to go," she said.

"Why?"

"I'll be seven months and don't want to chance it, so you go and hurry back to Mama."

That week, Trina went home. She was well rested and made her rounds to see everyone. That next morning, she met up with ten people that she had interviewed. They came highly recommended to work in a stockbroker company, Ken's company. There were eight men and two ladies that looked manly as Ken. Trina told them she needed everyone to come today around noon. They was ready to start working for Kenneth and Trina Brown.

Trina walked in the office and called a meeting.

"Ms. Simms, how are you?"

"I've been waiting to see you."

She went to hug Trina, but Trina backed up.

"Everyone, this way please," Trina said, "Ms. Simms, do you have all the reports and account card badges?"

She thought Trina was just taking count of everything.

Trina said, "I'll be right back." Trina called security up to the floor. She cancelled everyone on the list cards and badges. Trina walked back in and said, "As of now, I will no longer need any more of your services. I thank you. And your last check can be picked up at the door. Please go clean out your desk and leave the building.

Simms said, "What, you can't fire us! Only Kenneth can do that. I mean, Mr. Brown."

"No, you're wrong. I'm the head bitch of this company and what I say goes. Miss Simms, I need to see you."

Everyone walked out upset, looking at Simms, pissed off.

Trina sat down and said, "Simms, you fucking my husband?"

"No, Trina! Why would you asked that? I'm a smart woman."

"I'll tell you this, you can fuck him by all means, but you will not take food from me and mines. That apartment you have that my husband was paying for, no more. I guess you haven't received your letter yet."

"What letter?"

"Check your mail when you get home. Tick, tick, times running out. Let me tell you a little secret. I will never divorce my husband. So a hoe like yourself can have him, but like I said, by all means fuck him and suck him when he's in town. He maybe give you two hundred a night for your troubles." Trina laughed. "See, sweetie, I'm running shit, not Kenneth Brown. There's a new sheriff in town, and her name's Catrina. Wifey, baby mama, I'm hell on wheels, so don't test me. I'm not to be fucked with. Now get your nasty ass out my building."

Trina sat her phone on the desk and waited for Ken to call her. Trina got a call from the front lobby. It was her new staff members.

"Send them up, please."

She went out to tell the old staff, "Thank you, stay blessed."

Trina welcomed the new staff into the office.

She said, "Everyone please welcome our new staff members. I need to know if I need to dismiss anyone else from this building?"

Everyone stood quiet.

"All right, let's make some money."

Trina said, "Carl, I need you to order lunch for the staff, please. A little of everything because I'll be here all day and my baby's a little hungry as well."

"Okay, Mrs. Brown, I'm about to order it right now."

Once Mitch arrived, Trina sat down and said, "I need some separation papers drawn up, please."

"Are you serious?"

"Yes, I am."

They was adding Trina's name outside and also on the door.

"I want all these businesses to go to my children when they get twenty-one if something happens to me. Until they reach those ages, Greg will oversee them."

"So right now, Ken works for you."

She smiled. "I'll give him his share. I want five thousand for each child in support, and he can have them every other weekend, during the week between 4:00 to 7:00 p.m. I won't be nasty about anything. The money that he makes from Japan, I want my 50 percent and then he can get 50 percent, take it or leave it. The house in Japan, we can share. The house in Atlanta, that is all mine. And I want custody of my children."

"Trina, that won't be hard to do. But, Trina, you sure about this?"

"Yes, sir, so get to work on this. Ken will be out of town two more weeks then back there, and I want to be out of the house when he comes back. I need the paperwork done so I can leave them when I leave Japan."

"Yes, ma'am."

"Mrs. Brown, lunch has arrived."

"Mitch, let's go eat," she said.

Well, Ken had called Trina many times, but she wouldn't pick up the phone. Mitch left, and Trina went back in the office and changed some passwords. This time when Ken called, Trina picked up.

Ken yelled, "Have you fucking lost your mind, Trina?"

"No, not really. What's wrong, baby? Just made some adjustments at the business. We now have the best stockbrokers around. No more hair doing, nails, or clothes shopping up in here. Your dumb ass busy screwing these hoes, and they were taking from my child's mouth. Well, not anymore. Come on, talk, Kenneth. I have work to do."

"Bitch, you gone crazy? Trina, I need some money."

"I can't help you. Look two weeks, $200 a day, 7 days, and that's $2,800. Make it work."

"Trina, where's the cash? There's none in the safe," he said.

"I have it." Trina had taken the big black bag to her grandfather's to keep. "I'll see you next week."

"Trina. I will come there and beat the brakes off of you, baby or not."

"Yeah, that's what I want you to do. I'll tell Cleo to send you some money so you can get here. But remember this, Kenny…when you come, you better be ready for war." She hung up.

Trina called it a day and went to spend some time with her son.

Ken's mom called Trina.

"Yes, Ms. Gwen?"

"Trina, what's going on with you and Kenneth?"

"He called you. Why didn't he tell you everything? He's a liar and cheat. And I'm time enough for that ass."

"Trina, you can't keep all his money from him."

"Oh yes, I can. It's mines since he gave it to me. He has money, Ms. Gwen."

"Well, he's coming here, Trina. I just ordered the ticket."

"Okay, I'll be waiting."

"Trust and believe that."

Trina went and had dinner with Chris out in public and didn't care who saw them.

"You know this means war."

"Why? We just having dinner."

"Trina, you're a nut."

"I know that."

"So now what?"

"I don't know, Chris. I just want to relax, have my baby, and focus on me."

He said, "And me. I like this friend thing we got going on. So you moving to Atlanta?"

"Yes, right after my checkup, I'm heading south. So the pool you can do that."

"Yes, I will have it done. Pay me when you come to Atlanta. You paid for all the equipment, so that's all I need."

Ken couldn't even get on the private plane without Trina's permission.

She went home and went to bed.

That morning, she got up, fed KJ and said, "Mommy, Ken will be here, but don't let him take KJ anywhere."

Her dad said, "Ken not stupid. Crazy but not stupid."

Trina went to her shop and talked to Josh. All the orders in Japan was doing great for just being opened for three weeks.

"Okay now, I'm leaving, so I can go to Mr. Brown's place of business."

"Girl, please be careful."

"Always," she replied. "See you tonight at the club. Pick me up around nine o'clock, Josh."

"No, I'll be there at 8:00 p.m."

As she was leaving the shop, Ken sped up and jumped out and grabbed Trina by the hair.

"So we playing dirty, Trina?"

"Ken, let go of my hair."

Trina went for his dick and grabbed it hard.

"Trina, let go. You're hurting me."

"Let go of my hair."

Josh came out. "Kenneth, let her go, she's pregnant."

"I don't give a flying fuck!"

Josh had no choice but to call the police.

He finally let Trina loose and said, "Give me my money, Trina."

"Hell no!"

Ken smacked Trina in the face, and she went off on his ass.

Businessowners came out looking at them.

A man came up and asked, "Did you just smack her?"

"Mind your business. Trina, I want my money."

"Ken, fuck you."

The police officers came rolling in.

Trina said, "He hit me, and I want his ass locked up."

The man said, "He smacked the hell out of this young lady."

Trina's father came speeding up his car with her brother wanting to kick Ken's ass.

"Your wife's pregnant, and you slapped her?" Josh said.

Trina's father went off too. Trina had to apologize to all the business people around for what they had just seen.

Ken saw a buddy of his passing by and yelled, "Go by my father's and let him know I'm about to get locked up."

"Look at your face, Trina," her dad said.

"I'm okay."

She went back inside, got her purse, and went to the house.

Her father got there shortly after she did. "Llena, you were right. She has done it again. Pregnant by this nut. Trina, why? Please tell me why would you get pregnant again? And knowing all this in your marriage is going on. Tell me, Trina, why?"

"Daddy, not now!"

Trina booked a flight to Japan. She called Greg and said, "It's now or never, so tell Shelly to be ready. I need to leave now while they have Ken locked up. We leave 4:00 p.m. Mommy, I need you to go to Aunt Mae's house with KJ today. Don't tell Ken where you are. Daddy, I need you to call me if Ken gets out. I have my things being packed up as we speak. A moving truck will transfer my things to Atlanta. Timmy, I need you and Mel to go get all my belongs out of storage and take it to Atlanta." She gave him $1000. "Chris will help y'all leave today." Trina called Chris. "It needs to be done now." Trina kissed her son and said, "Mommy, if you love me, just please go get packed and leave."

"No, he will know I'm in Jersey or Virginia, Trina. I'll go to my girlfriends in DC."

Her father turned and looked at her and told her, "You and Ken need to be done with."

Trina went up and changed her clothes.

She got a call from Ken's lawyer and he said, "Trina, listen to me. I will have Ken sign the papers if you don't press charges. If you don't come to court when he needs to be there."

"I can do all of that if he stay away from me and KJ until we both cool off. But if he does anything dumb, I will sing like a bird on him about everything, and I mean everything I know and saw."

"Okay, so when will he have access to his money?"

"He has an account that I will release to him that has $2 million in it. That's all he will get but not until he signs and it gets in my lawyer's hand and I get the call. So you better get to steppin'.

"I'm on it, Trina. Thanks."

"Trina, he wants to see Kenneth Jr."

"No, not until I have everything I need in my lawyer's hand and we both have cooled off. So tell him in a couple days. I will have my parents call him. And he will sign a paper that KJ doesn't leave out the States without my consent."

"Yes, ma'am."

Trina hang up. "Mommy take my truck."

Greg pulled up and said, "Let's go."

She said, "KJ, Mommy loves you."

"Trina, please take your pills."

"I will, Mommy." Trina grabbed a bottle of water and hopped in the truck with Greg. "We need to go get Shelly."

"You okay?"

"Yes."

"Look at your damn face. Ken did that?"

"Yes, he slapped me. He locked up for now until he signs every piece of paper Mitch sent his lawyer."

"Trina, this not about the money. Trina, this is about you got him by the balls, and he know it."

Shelly came out and said, "We out, Trina. Girl, you be getting it in hard with your hubby."

"Shelly he hit me so hard I had to stand there for a minute, but when I came back, I was on that ass."

"Trina was like tazmania."

"Was I? Greg, I hope you ready to be my roommate again."

"Trina girl, I'm ready. Ken better not come down with that shit."

Shelly said, "The house looks really nice."

Greg told Trina, "She was about to take your bedroom, but I didn't want no trouble."

"It's going to take like a week for all my things to get to me."

"It's not much, right?"

"No, just clothes but I need to go get everything I'm taking back with me."

Trina called her father and told him to pick up the RV tomorrow. "It's already paid for. Daddy, I love you."

"I love you, Trina. You just be doing some dumb shit."

Trina called her grandfather and told him, "In the morning, take the money to the bank and deposit it, but keep $20,000 for yourself and $10,000 out for me."

All three were onboard the plane, and Trina had taken her pills so she would sleep most the way there.

Greg said, "I'm glad she had the private plane coming back."

Ken was released that evening after he signed all the papers Trina wanted from him. He got out.

"She wants full custody of the kids? That's some fucked up shit. But it's all good. I'll see my son when I'm supposed to once I get back, Dad. No problem."

"Kenneth, what made her do all this?"

Ken looked at his father.

"No...Kenneth."

"Yes and, Dad, I really don't want to hear it right now."

His father dropped him at the rental truck. He said, "I'll see you in a little bit."

Ken went and had a drink with Cleo. He ran into Chris as he was pulling into the gas station.

He looked at Ken and smiled.

"Hey, Chris, you seen Trina?"

"She's your wife. Don't you know where she is?"

"You punk ass, you know."

"Let me get your ass back to your parents' house," Leo said. "You need to stay out of trouble."

Trina arrived in Japan after a long flight. She got there, but Mrs. Suki wasn't there and neither was Sue.

Greg said, "Nice."

The movers took everything of Trina's and KJ's. Trina suitcases was packed and ready. Her grandfather came over with the money and so did her cousins.

"Ken will be coming back, but here's a key. I know he will reach out to you, Papa."

"I will come to visit you soon."

"You better, Papa," Trina said. She turned to her cousins. "Tye and Boogie, I need you to keep this shop running, and I will check in every week."

"We got you and the shop," they both replied.

Trina locked the house up, and they left with four big suitcases. She told the driver to take her to the airport where she went through the process before getting on the private plane. She was so glad when they left the airport.

Trina called her mom. KJ was okay, bad as always.

"Trina, Ken called and he just asked how was his son doing? Trina, you can't keep him from seeing his son."

"I'll have you call him."

"I already did, and he's coming to see him in a few."

"Okay, Mom. I'll talk to you later," Trina said. "My mom always taking Ken's side. All he needs to do is give her that sad story and she falls for it."

Ken came over and spent the evening with his son.

"Mama Lena, I do want to apologize. I shouldn't have touched Trina, and I will tell her that also."

"Yes, you do that 'cause he is your son and that unborn child is too. And you should never mistreat her or any woman. You hungry a little?" she asked. She fixed him a plate, and he fed KJ.

"Mama Lena, I love this little boy so much. I don't want Trina to take him from me."

"She won't, Ken. But I think it's time for you and Trina to give it a rest."

"She can rest all she wants. I'm not giving her a divorce."

"And why the hell not?"

"Mr. Billy, I'm not giving up on Trina. We just need to take a break and try this again. We rushed into this marriage too fast. I want to get to know my wife again. I'll let her do her for now, but she'll be back to Daddy."

"You got it bad. But, Ken, if you ever put your hands on my daughter again, I'll break those legs. You got it?"

"Yes, sir. That shouldn't have happen. But she grabbed my private area and wouldn't let go."

"I don't give a flying fuck." He slapped him upside the head. "You see my grandson?"

"Yes."

"That's you, Kenneth. Do you want him to grow up beating on women?"

"No, sir."

"Case closed."

A knock came at the door.

"Come in."

It was Chris.

"What's up Mrs. Lena, how are you doing today?"

"I'm doing okay."

"Kenneth, man, don't say nothing to me."

Her mom asked, "Why y'all hate each other so much?"

"I don't hate Kenneth," Chris replied. "I just don't like how he treats me and Trina!"

"Man, you don't know shit."

"I know you just lost your wife. I know you put your hands on her today. And it's not sitting with me very well right now. Look, me and Trina have history, and you or no other will come between that. So listen real good, Kenneth. I'm there for Trina for anything, and I mean anything."

Ken laughed. "And I want you to remember what I said a while back," he said, winking his eye at Chris. "So you have your fun for now. But she'll be back to Daddy. And my son only has one father, so stop all that playing that role. Don't go there with mine."

They was going back in forth.

"*Enough!*" Lena said. "Ken, finish feeding your son."

Billy came down and gave him the keys.

"Okay, I'm gone, Mr. Billy. Tell Trina to call me."

"I will."

"Thanks. Timmy left?"

"Yes, about an hour ago."

"Okay."

"Trina went to Atlanta?"

"No, she'll be in here tonight or sometime in the morning."

"I'm leaving tomorrow night, so I need to talk to Trina before I go. Can someone please have her call me?"

"I'll let her know."

Ken finally left and went to his parents' house.

His mom asked him, "Now what you going to do?"

"I'm going out, and I'll be back later. Tomorrow I'm going to say bye to my son and have a talk with his mother without choking the hell out of her—or sticking this size eleven and a half up her big ass. Then I'm going back to Japan so I can make this money and at least get my 50 percent from my company," Kent said.

"My sister-in-law socked it to you, dumb ass."

"Kent, not now. I already got one charge against me. I don't need another. Later," he said and walked out the house.

He drove over to Simm's house, and she opened the door. He walked in and went in the bedroom.

"I need to be out in two weeks."

"So what you want me to do?"

"Can't you go and cancel this shit Trina did."

"No, I can't, Simms. Just go back to your moms. I'm going back to Japan in the morning. I shouldn't have never start fucking with you. I would have my family in Japan with no worries."

"I'm sorry I do the job better than your wife."

"You may suck dick good, but you will never please me like my wife in no kind of way. I just can't say no to you bitches." He takes his clothes off. "Now bring your fucking ass over here and give me what I need to get my mind off my wife."

Simms had two abortions, and they both belonged to Ken. She got a her tubes tied, like a dummy, believing Ken would be with her.

Ken lay back in the bed and enjoyed her blow job. He fucked the hell out of Simms and was calling out Trina's name. Ken deals with these hoes just for busting nuts and then leaving. That's what he does best.

Ken got dressed and said, "See you around," smiling.

He told her, "Cleo will be over in a couple of days to get all the stuff out the condo."

"What I'm going to do about a bed, Kenneth?"

"Don't know, don't care." He walked out and went back over his parents' house to take a shower. While lying in bed, he kept thinking about Trina.

Shelly told Greg that she was tired.

"This has been the longest fucking ride of my life, Shelly."

"Greg, I know."

"Trina can have this ride alone."

They finally got back early that morning and dropped Trina off.

Greg said, "See you tonight. Text me what time we pulling out, okay?"

"See you later, Shelly."

"I'll be going also."

"Stop playing, Shelly. Later, Trina."

Trina looked, seeing the RV gone and went in the house.

"Look who came back to you."

"Hey, son. Kiss me, boyfriend."

He laughed.

"Greg has my suitcases. You got everything?"

"Call Ken."

"I will."

"Trina, he's leaving today, so call him."

"Let's go take a bath, stinky butt."

Trina went upstairs, and she and the little man got in the tub. She called Ken.

He said, "Trina?"

"Yes, I'm home. Can we talk?"

"Sure, I'm on my way now."

Trina blew bubbles at KJ.

"Trina, you eating not right now? KJ's bottle's on the nightstand."

"Thank you, Mommy."

The doorbell rang.

"Hey, Mommy, that's Ken."

"Who is that?" Grandma Lena said.

"Say Daddy."

Ken came in, saying, "Good morning."

"Morning, Ken."

"They are upstairs in the tub."

"Can I go up?"

"Yes, she didn't say you couldn't."

So he did, calling Trina's name out loud.

"We in the bathroom."

"What, you giving him a bath?" Then he saw Trina was in the water with him.

"KJ, stop before you go under, boy!"

Ken said, "Hey, chill, son."

He showed off, seeing his father there.

Ken got a towel and took him out the tub. He also handed Trina a towel, helping her up out the tub.

"Your stomach's big with baby girl."

"Yes, very much."

Ken took KJ and got him dried off and put his Pampers on.

Trina said, "He can just wear a T-shirt."

Her mom came upstairs. "KJ, you ready to eat, so you can go back to sleep with Nana? Come on. Trina, do this boy hair today."

"I will, Mommy."

Ken sat down and asked Trina if he could take KJ over his mom's to spend some time with him before he left tonight.

"Yes. Don't take my son over no one's house, Kenneth."

"Trina, I want to apologize for hitting you. I'll never do that again."

Trina just looked at him.

"Trina, I think it's best we go our separate ways."

"I agree."

Ken told Trina, "I am not giving you a divorce. It's not happening. When I get back, I want to try this again. As friends first and see where it goes. I mean, we'll have two kids soon. I know we rushed this marriage, but now I know we should have waited. I don't regret my son or my daughter, Trina. So tell whoever when Daddy's in town. I will be with my family. I'm leaving tonight."

"Ken, I'm going to Atlanta."

He shut the door, and he held Trina, kissing her softly. "I'm so sorry for all that I've put you through. I'm going to make it right."

He made love to his wife one last time. Trina found herself weak when it comes to Ken. The love-hate for each other was unbelievable.

Ken said, "Get some rest." He got dressed and then got KJ dressed too. Ken took his son with him to spend time together before they parted ways.

That evening everyone waited for Ken to bring KJ so they could leave. He finally got there with bags of clothes and toys. They had both eaten.

"That's what took us so long," he said.

"Thanks."

"Shelly, can you take KJ, please?" Ken told his son, "I will miss you," kissing him on his fat cheeks. He had tears in his eyes. "Trina, please call me, if my son or if anything going on I should know about."

"I will, Kenneth."

"I will try to be back at the end of July until you have baby girl." He kissed her on the forehead and left. "Daddy, take me home, please."

Ken went and got ready to go back to Japan. Trina sent him a picture of his son, saying, "Dada." and throwing kisses.

He laughed and said, "Thank you. So, Dad, you ready to take me to the airport? Cleo's meeting me there to fly back with me."

That morning Trina was in landing in Atlanta and Ken was about to hit Japan with his best friend.

"Oh wow, look at my house. It's so pretty."

"Trina, I'm glad you kept your grandfather's house the same in the front."

"Yes, Mommy, that old-stone look."

Timmy, Mel, and Chris worked hard getting everything into place for Trina before she got there.

"Thank y'all so much." Chris, you wasn't playing driving the RV here.

"Nope."

"Trina, this house is too big for just you and Greg."

"No, it's not."

"Trina keep having all these damn kids, it will fill up real soon."

Chris said, "I'm on that list, right?"

"What?"

KJ reached for Chris.

"Hey, KJ, what's wrong? You in a strange place?"

Timmy told his father, "Boy, if Ken seen this right here, he would go off."

"Yes, Lawd!" Billy said.

"You want to see your rooms."

Tina and Chris went up to see the rooms.

"Oh my Lawd, I love it."

"Timmy did it himself. Nice, isn't it?

"KJ, who's that on your wall" Trina said.

It was a picture of Trina and Ken with baby KJ.

"I love it." Trina took a video of KJ's room and sent it to Ken.

Chris went back down and left them upstairs making a video for Ken.

Trina said, "Let's show Daddy what's on your wall. This right here is life, Kenneth Brown, your son here with me and…" She showed him her stomach. "So, yes, we need to work this out slowly. But this isn't fair to me or our son. You think about that long and hard." She ended her video and said, "Come on, KJ."

KJ sat waiting for Trina to pick him up. Then they went back down, joining everyone.

Ken received his video and cried while lying in his bed. He watched it over and over until he fell asleep. Ken just couldn't sleep, wanting to call Trina up, but he didn't do it. He just lay there fighting the feelings he was having to pack up and go fight for what was his, but he knew that right at this moment, it wouldn't be a good time to do so.

Trina felt right at home, enjoying her granddaddy's house.

"Trina, daddy's house felt really good, being here."

"I know, Mommy, I feel him here with me. I was hoping that this one was a boy so I could name him after granddaddy. But her name will be Natalee Nicole."

"Have you talked to Kenneth about that, Trina?"

"No."

"You should."

"Mommy, why he doesn't love me like I love him?"

"Trina, men can be so hard on the outside and soft on the insides. Ken loves you, Trina, but he hasn't grown up yet. Maybe this will open his eyes. And having a little girl may help."

"I mean, I work, cook, clean…and I know I do my part in the bedroom. I just don't get it, Mommy."

"Well, a few months apart may help. But then you have Chris that wants to be with you also."

"Mommy, he wants a child with me, not a relationship."

"Oh, he wants you."

"Hey, Trina!"

"Yes?"

"We going to get something to eat, you going?"

"No. Take KJ with you, Daddy."

"Lena, let's roll."

Chris came up and asked, "Trina, you okay?"

"Yes. Thank you for helping."

"No problem. I'll be pass next weekend to work on the pool."

"Thanks."

"Call me later."

"I will. Be safe, Chris."

Trina picked up her phone and pressed Ken's number, then hung up.

A few months have passed, and Trina was now on her eighth month of pregnancy. Ken was coming to town to stay close to Trina since she had been having problems with this pregnancy. He had gotten a hotel suite to stay in. Ken had finished his project in Japan and wanted to focus on getting his family back. Ken hadn't seen his son since they went back to the States. KJ was now one year old and walking, just as spoiled as ever.

When Ken arrived at the house around Trina's birthday, he had bags of gifts for his son and his wife. Ken couldn't get in any trouble, so he had to play it cool with Trina and anyone else or he was looking at jail time. For a year, he had to play nice.

Trina said, "KJ, who's that walking up to the door?"

He smiled, looking at his dad, and walked toward the door.

Trina opened the door, and Ken picked KJ up, dropping everything. He held him so tight, tears falling from his eyes. Ken walked outside with him, holding him tightly, saying, "Oh, Kenneth Jr., I have missed you so much. Daddy will never leave you again."

He looked at Ken, touching his face.

"Yes, it's me, Dada."

KJ laid his head on his father's shoulder.

Trina stood there with tears of joy that Ken was there with his son.

"Kenneth Jr., let me see these legs everybody keep talking about." He put him down. He was Ken's son and bow-legged just like him. "Your mom may have carried you, but got damn, I marked you well."

"It's like you were never gone, Ken."

He turned to hug Trina and said, "Happy Birthday."

"Thank you."

He got the gifts, and they went inside the house.

"Wow, Trina this is nice. So how you feel?"

"Today's a good day so far."

He touched her stomach. "So where's Greg?"

"He's at his restaurant. He'll be back in a few. He's picking up the food, and we're cooking out today. Shelly's in the kitchen, she and Calvin."

"Where's your boyfriend?"

"Which one? Christopher?" she asked. "He's at work, and he's not my boyfriend."

"Not yet," Ken said.

"Chris has a girlfriend, and he does come to check on us when he can."

"Just checking, Trina?" Ken said. "Here, open your gift."

She sat down and opened the gift. It was a bathing suit.

"Ken, what is this?"

"Open the gifts, Trina."

A white sundress.

"Do you want to tell me what's this all about?"

"You, me, and a trip to the Bahamas after you have the baby."

"Just a trip."

"Now, whatever happens there, it's all good. So when you can travel, we'll go. Since Shelly's staying here, we have a babysitter."

"I have a nanny," Trina said. "Greg's girl, Becky. She's my assistant and nanny. She lives here with Greg."

"Come on." He helped her up. "That ass still phat to death."

"KJ, where girlfriend at?" Ken smiled, watching his son walk.

"Becky Boo, here's KJ's father, Ken."

"Oh wow, that's his twin!"

"Yes, I told you."

"Nice to meet you."

"What's up, Shelly? Calvin, my man?"

They hugged, then stood talking shit.

"Trina, sit down."

"Shelly, I'm about to."

"Okay, didn't they tell you if you come back to the hospital again, you're staying?"

"What hospital?"

"Thanks, Shelly," Trina replied.

"When did you go to the hospital again?"

"Well, two days ago I picked KJ up and I started having pains."

"Trina, you can't be picking him up," Ken said. "He can walk."

KJ said, "Baby," touching his mother's stomach.

"Yes, son, baby sister." Ken picked him up and went to go look at the house. "Hey, Trina, where's my room at?"

"My room's down the hall and up those few steps. KJ's room's up the stairs, and now you can pick one of the guest rooms."

"You must be on crack, Trina." Calvin laughed.

"Man, she don't know, does she?"

"I guess not, Ken. She still wearing those wedding rings."

Ken then said, "She knows Daddy's back in town."

"Shelly, don't you laugh at him."

"I haven't been with a woman in four months."

"Oh, Ken, stop lying."

"Trina, why do I need to lie to you? Come see."

"No, I'm good."

"I bet you are."

"Ken, everybody's not like you. Bye, Kenneth."

Trina's mom and dad pulled up.

Trina asked, "Who's that? Oh, Lawd, it's my parents!" Trina went and let them in.

Greg was rolling in also.

"Mommy and Daddy, you said you couldn't come until next week."

"We lied."

She kissed them.

"Kenneth here?"

"Yes."

Her father said, "It's about time he brought his ass back to his son."

"Yes, because a sister needs a break."

"Don't we all?" said Shelly. "Now Kenneth Brown can do the footwork and the runs to the store."

"Shelly, it's a bitch. At 2:00 a.m. in the morning, she is crying for a damn cupcake. Look, KJ be up eating with her."

Ken came back down, smiling. He said Trina, "What side do I sleep on?"

Her mother choked, drinking a soda. "Greg, can you put the steaks on, please?"

"Daddy, where's brother at?"

"He's doing ten days in the detention center?"

Everybody said, "What!"

"Yes, didn't pay his support on time, and when he did, they still locked him up. He better hope he still got a job when he gets out."

Ken went outside and sat down to talk to Greg about Trina.

"Ken, she's been having problems for a couple months. I told her I was going to tell you."

"Trina, can you come outside please, pretty please?"

"What's up, Ken?"

"Sit down," he said, smacking on his leg. "Girl, sit down."

"What, Ken?" she said, sitting down on his lap.

"So why didn't you tell me you been having problems with this pregnancy? You made it seem like you just started having problems a week ago."

"It was stress, Ken, that's all."

He took his shades off and just looked at Trina. "So Natalee, Nicole, she's okay? Now what can I call my daughter?"

"Lee, that's what I'm going to call her," Trina said to Ken.

"I guess that's what we'll both call her." Ken kissed Trina's round belly. "I missed you and KJ so much."

"Can we talk, please?"

"Let's go inside."

Trina and Ken walked back inside and went in her room.

He said, "I have done a lot of thinking, and I know we have a lot of work to do. I want to work on us slowly. So have our daughter, then we will date and get to know each other all over again. Deal?"

"Deal," Trina said.

"Now can we seal with a kiss."

Then they kissed.

He said, "Can I stay over tonight, just a stay over? If not, I understand."

"Yes, KJ would like that."

"How about lil' mama?"

"Umm, I guess I would also."

"Now we ready to eat. Ken, stop looking at my ass."

"I can't. Miss it."

"What's wrong with KJ? He's been looking for you."

Ken picked him up and said, "Tomorrow you are going to get a haircut."

Trina sat and ate until she couldn't eat no more.

That night Ken bathed KJ and lay with him in his room until he went to sleep.

Becky said, "Trina, it feels good, doesn't it? Just to relax without running around, trying to put KJ to bed."

"Yes, it does," she replied.

"Well, good night."

"Do you need anything?"

"No, I better not eat another thing."

Trina had on a short T-shirt and panties, sitting in bed propped on a pillow and putting her hair in a French braid. Ken came up with his bag and took his shower. Trina waited and then checked Ken's phone. He had a few messages from Nikki. He was telling her that he was trying to get his wife back, just talking in general. There wasn't no other calls. Trina put his phone back down, but she noticed he didn't have a code on his phone.

Ken came out and said, "Trina, pink, really?"

"I love pink. Everything's pink in the bathroom."

He lotioned down and put on some oil. Ken dropped the towel and got in the bed, kissing Trina good night. He kissed her belly again. Ken turned off his light.

Trina said, "Ken."

"Yes, wifey."

"I haven't been with anyone. I just wanted to tell you that.

"I know you haven't," he said. "Come on. Come, lie on Daddy like old times."

"Ken, you know what?"

"What, Trina?" He smiled.

"I just can't get you out my system. I try, but you're like a bug prick that just stick to you and draw the blood without you even knowing."

"So, wifey, what do you do with that kind of bug?"

"I already did, and you still keep coming back."

"And what was that?"

"I burned the hell out your cheating ass. But I also learned something with you, Kenneth. You need to hit where it would hurt. I will never put your children in the middle of our battles, but trust and believe me, I won't be this time, you will."

"See, Trina, you messing this great vibe we got going on. Can you please just lie here and enjoy Daddy's back? Trina, touch it."

"What!"

"Touch it like you used too."

Trina lifted the cover and said, "Why you hard? And why you look bruised?"

"Girl, you would be all beat up too if hands been on you, choking the neck two, three times a day for four months straight."

Trina was tickled to death.

He said, "Come on, Trina." He was begging her, so she played with it and kissed it gently.

Ken moved. "You fucked that up. But it was worth a try, wifey."

He removed Trina's panties and shirt, rubbed his soft hands on her body and started kissing her from head to toe. "I missed you so much." He opened her up wide as he entered her warm pussy and released his warm nut inside of her. "Wifey, I told you so." He kissed her lips so gentle, and Trina was on fire from not having sex. She wanted him so bad.

Ken said, "Shhh, before you wake up the house!"

Trina got on top and held her stomach as she was riding Ken up and down, up and down.

He went, "Damn girl...wifey, slow down. Be gentle."

She was manhandling that dick like she was shifting gears.

Ken held his head, moaning. "Baby, I'm about to explode."

"Please cum inside, Daddy. Right now," she sighed.

He grabbed on to her ass and released everything in him. "Trina, you wasn't that horny with KJ. And we have had beef while you were pregnant with him."

"Well, Ken, it wasn't four month either."

He asked, "Does Kenneth Jr. sleep all night?"

"No, he's just like you, an early bird. He'll be up around 5:00 a.m. or 6:00 a.m."

"Are you serious?"

"Very. I know you be mad. I curse you out every day, Ken Brown."

He lay down and held Trina close.

While Trina slept, he lay watching his daughter move around in her mother's belly. Ken could actually see his baby's little butt as she doubled up inside Trina. He woke Trina up.

"Babe, wake up?"

"What's wrong?

"I see her butt."

"Whose butt?

"Baby girl's."

"Ken, you woke me up for that?" she asked.

"Trina, look!"

"Yes, she's been out partying, Ken. Now she ready to go to bed like her mom. Double up in a spot and sleep after a full meal at the club and a good lay."

"Trina, you funny. I pray my daughter's a good girl."

"Hell, I was a good girl until I met your sneaky conniving ass. And if she looks like me, built like me, and act like me, then she'll be clocking like me."

"Trina, I don't want to hear that shit," he said.

Trina got up and went to the bathroom, laughing to herself. "I'm hungry, Ken."

"Yeah, me too."

KJ was up yelling and making noise.

"Listen to his rude ass." Ken slipped on his pajamas and went and got him.

Trina pulled the sheet up and said, "Son, good morning."

He was looking at his father like, "What the hell's going on?"

Ken told him, "Yes, Daddy's here. Let's get changed and go downstairs."

"Here's his pull-up, Ken, and his pot is downstairs. He know what to do. Show Daddy your pot."

KJ ran to her bathroom, pointing.

"Now when you get downstairs, ask him to show you his pot."

Trina lay in bed, relaxing. "Call me when breakfast fixed."

Ken took his son down, asking him, "Show me potty."

He pointed again.

"So that means no pull-up when you get dressed. You going to get a haircut."

KJ felt his hair and shook his little head no.

"Kenneth, Daddy back now, and we get haircuts today."

He was walking around in circles saying, "Eat, eat."

"Okay. Now what do your mother fix you in the morning?" he said, talking to himself.

Shelly came in the kitchen. "Good morning, KJ. What you doing acting crazy like Trina?"

Ken said, "What the hell does she fix him?"

"That boy eats everything Trina eats."

Ken started cooking, fixing KJ some oatmeal for breakfast. "Look at your greedy self."

Becky came in next and asked Ken if he needed some help. "Can you go get Trina up for me, please?"

"Sure."

KJ started yelling, "Bee, bee, bee."

Ken fixed Trina's plate and said, "Shelly, you and Calvin eating?"

"Yes."

KJ was pigging out.

"Trina's coming, Ken."

"Okay, thanks. Wake Greg up so he can eat too."

"Everything looks and smells good. I hope it taste good."

Trina came down.

"Mommy!"

"Trina, why you yelling?"

"Because I need my mother."

Trina went to her room. Her father was half asleep.

Trina said, "Mommy, pink gel coming out my vajayjay."

"Got damnit, Trina, I really don't want to hear about your pregnant ass this early in the morning."

"Trina, it's okay. Call your doctor."

"I did. He hasn't called back yet."

"You having pain?"

"No, ma'am."

"That baby will let you know when she's coming."

"Ken cooked breakfast."

"That's why that ass is spotting."

"No, it's not, Daddy."

Trina went back over and sat down.

"What's wrong, Trina?"

"I'm spotting pink gel."

"Let's go to the hospital then."

"No, Kenneth. I called my doctor. He'll call back in a few, I'm sure."

"Becky, can you take KJ and get him ready 'cause he's going to get his haircut."

"Trina, you think it was too much last night?"

"Maybe. I told you to cool it."

"Shit, it was good. I saw baby girl getting in position."

Trina said, "Her head is down. Feel right here, Ken."

"Trina, she's coming."

"She better not come yet."

"Trina, if she's ready, she's going to come."

"But I'm not ready for her to come yet. I'm thirty-five weeks. God, please let her stay for a couple more weeks."

"Well, you better keep still."

Trina went upstairs as she couldn't eat.

Ken took his shower and said to Trina, "Go back to sleep."

Trina's doctor finally called before Ken had left out with KJ. The doctor told her it's normal and to just stay in bed and that if she had any pain, to call him right back."

Ken said, "He wouldn't be gone long at the Barbershop."

Chris called Trina to check on her, and she told him that Ken was in Atlanta, but Chris wasn't worried about Ken's ass at all.

"I see you tomorrow since I have a job near you. I'll stop by."

"Okay, Chris."

The house was quiet as Becky was fixing dinner. Ken had taken KJ to the hotel with him and got some more clothes to stay with Trina at the house. He knew it was matter of time before his daughter would arrive. He called his parents to let them know what was going on, and they wanted him to keep them posted. When Ken got back, Trina was eating and watching TV.

"KJ, where you been?"

He smiled.

"Aw, look at my baby's hair."

Ken had his braid in a Ziplock bag for Trina to keep. KJ was touching his head.

"All gone, KJ."

"Daddy also got a haircut."

"Wow," Trina said.

"Trina, how you feel?"

"Okay."

Greg came up in her room, saying, "Here, greedy ass."

"Thank you."

"Daddy, come here, please."

He decided to come to see what Trina wanted and said, "What, Trina?"

"Can you go get me a snowball, please."

"Trina, I asked your wide ass did you want anything while I was out, and what did you say? 'No, not at the moment.'"

Ken laughed.

"Gotdamn, Trina. Ken, your baby daddy, husband, whatever he is right now, he's sitting next to you."

"Wifey, what kind of snowball you want?"

"Mint please."

So Ken went and got his wife a snowball. He was doing whatever to please her.

With Trina and Greg in the kitchen acting crazy, her favorite song comes on and she was getting it, just dancing.

Her mom said, "Now that's a hot mess, I tell you."

"KJ, show Nana you can dance."

He was rocking side to side.

Ken walked in, looking at him. "What the hell."

"That's all the time, Ken. You haven't seen shit yet."

Trina yelled, "*Hey…hey…hey…* Go, KJ. Go, KJ, go, go, go." She smiled as he danced around in a circle.

"Trina, you should sit down."

"I am 'cause the baby's kicking now. This little brat, she's sassy as hell." Trina sat and enjoyed her snowball, sharing it with her son. "I think I'm going to take a swim after KJ goes to bed."

Greg said, "Yeah, lets hit the pool."

"When did the pool get finished?"

Trina told him, "A couple months ago. Chris and his friends did it for me."

"How much he charge you, Trina?"

"Nothing. I just fix them all dinner."

Ken said, "Whatever!"

Trina smiled. "Mommy, I want you to look at this baby blanket that Shelly's mom sent me." Trina went to go get it.

"Trina, are you finished eating, yet?"

"Yes, Becky. KJ, what you crying for?"

Becky said, "He wants another roll."

Trina said, "One more, greedy."

"Trina, don't give him a lot of bread."

"Look who talking, Kenneth."

"Son, go with girlfriend." He was holding himself. "Kenneth Jr., you need to potty?"

He walked to his pot, and he could pull his underwear down by himself. KJ sat looking at his pee go in his potty and started clapping. Ken was so happy seeing all this.

"I'm so glad to see my son." He was talking to Mama Lena.

Ken's phone rang, and it was Cleo. "What's up, bro?"

"Man, Trina not ready to have no baby yet. She needs to hold out until my birthday. The Fourth of July's a week away."

"Trina, you having a cookout?"

"Yes. Tell Cleo he better come."

"You heard her, right?"

"Mitch and Lisa coming. Chris and Val are also coming."

Ken said, "Really, Trina?"

"Yes, really."

Becky took KJ up for his bath, and she brought him back down to say good night. He got his cup filled with milk and went up for bedtime. Trina went upstairs and put on her bathing suit.

Her father said, "There should be a law for a pregnant woman with a big ass to wear a two piece. Trina between your ass and that stomach, tsk, tsk, tsk."

"Daddy, feel her moving. She's moving toward the birth tunnel."

"Ken, you swimming?"

"No, you go ahead. I'm still trying to picture me and Chris at a cookout together."

"Play nice, Ken."

"Trina, you can say that, but let me do some crazy shit like that to you."

Trina jumped in the pool and went swimming. Her father got in and did a few laps with her. Greg and Calvin were sitting, firing up the blunt.

Ken said, "Let me hit that, so I can make Trina's water break tonight."

"Hey, Trina. Ken's talking shit over here."

Trina just kept on swimming. She got out and said, "I'm going to be pinching Ken's nipple." She laughed.

Greg laughed too. "Man, you in like Flynn."

"You think so, Greg?"

"The way she grabbed that nipple."

"Trina's horny. She is just using me for sex. After she have baby girl, Trina with be on a roll. Trust me with that motherfucken Chris. Watch and see. So I can break her neck."

"Ken, what you're going to do?"

"Break her neck and stick foot all in her big ass."

Calvin and Greg was laughing so hard.

"Shit, I owe her an ass kicking, and she knows it."

"Ken, man, don't fuck her up. You know Trina like busting windows and shooting at you."

"Trina's a crazy bitch, but I can get crazy with her. I know I love her.

Well, everyone, I'm out. Good night." Ken went up to check on his son and kissed him good night, then went in the bedroom where Trina's hot ass was lying out naked and rubbing her belly. Ken said, "You're a damn mess."

"Ken, she kicking hard. She's up now. Sleep all day and up all night."

Ken rubbed Trina's stomach and told her, "Trina, you know I don't mind being here, but don't just use me, then throw me away."

"I may keep you around, but I like this apart thing we had going on."

"Don't worry, I'm home to stay. So when can I come home?" he asked.

"Let me see what happens in six months, then I'll let you know."

"So I need to get it under control is what you're saying?"

Trina replied, "I'm saying get your shit together, or I'll be the worst baby mama, wifey you ever laid eyes on."

"Trina, let's not get dumb, okay?"

"No, baby, it's being smart. Trust and believe that."

"Now enough about how I can check your fine ass," he said while pulling on his pants. "Trina, you know how to make a person feel cheap at times."

"Boy, bye!" Trina was hot in the covers and said, "Kenneth, what you doing?"

"I'm going to get a drink."

"Ken!"

He walked out. Trina had hurt his feeling, saying all she said to him. Ken went and had a few drinks while sitting in his truck, just thinking should he forget everything and walk away from Trina or work on his marriage.

Trina came outside in a long shirt and asked Ken why was he in the truck.

"Trina, I'm just sitting here. Go to bed you need to rest."

"Ken, what you want me to do?"

"Nothing. You said everything you had to say. I fuck up. You'll fuck a motherfucker, and keep it moving."

"Ken, that's not what I said. But I deserve to be happy, and if my own husband can't keep me happy, then I need to move on. I love you so much, Ken, but you drain me. I lost weight when I came here. My hair was falling out. I had to make myself get out of bed each day, and the only thing got me up was our son. Now I'm going to bed. Good night. I'll see you in the morning."

She got out, and he started his truck up and rolled out.

Trina went in the house to sleep, believing Ken went for a ride.

When Trina woke up and he wasn't there, she went downstairs and Greg was on the sofa. Trina told Greg she would be right back and listen out for KJ.

"Where you going?"

"Over Ken's," she said.

Trina went over to the hotel and knocked on the door. It took him a minute to open the door. When he did, Trina pushed him out the way.

Ken said, "Girl, what's wrong with you?"

Trina went to look in the bathroom, open the closets, asking, "Where the bitch at, Kenneth?"

"Trina, what are you talking about?"

Trina looked under the bed too.

"Trina, there's no one in my suite."

"Why you leave then?"

"Trina, chill."

She started hitting him with her hand balled up.

"Trina, chill out." He laughed. "Look, I left because I wasn't trying to piss you off or fight with you. There's no one here. Stop. Please sit down, Trina." He got her a cup of water. "Stop before you'll at the hospital. I said stop. "Got damn." I'm not cheating on you. Who got my son? Greg? Let's go."

Ken grabbed his keys, and they left. He followed Trina back to the house and helped her out her truck. Ken walked in, went upstairs to look in on KJ and then went back down to Trina's bedroom. He got undress and got in bed. Trina came in the room and sat on the bed.

She said, "Ken, I will try this one last time for six months. If this doesn't work, it's over."

"Come to bed, Trina."

She got in bed, and they lay in each other's arms. He told her that he couldn't believe she came to the hotel. "Wait, I'm talking about my wife, Trina. You need to stop acting crazy."

"Look, you're my husband and my children's father. I'll beat a bitch ass, okay? And then yours."

"Down girl, you to hyped up this time of morning."

Trina got on top of Ken.

"Baby, you sure we should be doing it?" he asked.

"Yes, you just keep doing me until I can't take it anymore."

He kissed Trina. She was one horny, pregnant woman in her eighth month, and she meant business.

That week and a half was a stressful time for Ken, working from the hotel and Trina's, helping with KJ, killing him with all the sex; and he was drained. He found himself staying at the hotel to get rest from Trina. Trina went to Ken's hotel, and he was having a business meeting on the phone. He opened the door, and she had lunch for them. Ken gave her a kiss. She sat down, taking her sandals off. Then Trina walked over to Ken, who was sitting on the sofa with just his briefs on and no shirt. Trina got on top his lap kissing his neck. Ken tapped that ass, telling her to stop. He was trying to listen and answer questions with a client. He began to moan as Trina went down on him.

He said, "I will get back with you in twenty-four hours. Thank you very much for taking time out of your busy schedule so we could talk." He couldn't wait to hang up. "Baby, shit!" He pulled his briefs off and laid out as Trina took care of him. He was so loud, saying, "Oh, Trina, fuck! That feels some kind of good." She came up for air. He looked at Trina and said, "You having her tonight 'cause I'm about to beat the hell out of that pregnant pussy." He picked Trina up and took her in the room, and he put it down. He slapped that ass, tossed that ass, then ate the ass!

"You miss this, baby?"

"Yes, Daddy." He pulled out. "Don't you cum yet."

She was hotter than a firecracker lit in July. He was teasing Trina, but he let her get a few off, then he bust a big one inside her.

Ken told Trina, "No more. I'm empty now."

"Look at him, he dead, can't move, no life left in him."

"Whatever."

"You ready to go pick these crabs up?"

"Yes, so I can have fun with all your old boyfriends."

"Ken, please don't start."

"I'm not baby. We been doing great, so I'm sorry."

Ken and Trina took a shower and left. Trina drove her truck to the house, and they picked up Becky and Greg.

"What took y'all so long? Wait. Never mind."

She was looking at Ken's face.

Greg shook his head and told him, "Your dick has seen his days in the last couple weeks."

"Yes, indeed. I thought I would never say this, but I'm tired of fucking."

"Well, I'm about to get a boyfriend and let him do the work," Becky said. "Oh wow, little Kenneth's wiener is bigger than mine's right now. It has been sucked and fucked to death."

Trina laughed so hard with Greg and Becky.

Ken said, "Laugh but the shit isn't funny at all. Trina, does your father really know his precious daughter's a freak? I forgot, Mama Lena's one also. I heard them when we were living back home. Oh, Billy was tearing that big ass up. Mommy said, '*I love it…I love it*!'"

They all laughed.

"Where's KJ?"

"In the backyard with Billy."

"Good, let's go."

Trina said, "Ummm…"

"What's wrong?"

"Nothing, just baby girl kicking."

"Kent and Kim coming?"

"Yes, they're here. They went to the mall, Ken."

"Baby, why didn't you tell me?"

"Sorry, I was busy, and it wasn't on my mind." Trina said. "I'm ready to get these crabs now."

Ken was stopped at the red light and asked for some sugar. Trina smiled and leaned over, kissing him.

"Oh, Lawd, come on with all that. This relationship we have is a love-hate kind of love. That's what we got, baby."

"Yes, very much so."

"Well, I need to work on that," she said.

Getting to the crab spot, Trina talked trash to the old guy, and he gave her bushel and a half of crabs. She just paid for a bushel though.

Trina asked, "Can I also get three dozen of crab legs?" smiling at the old man.

"He needs to sit his old ass down somewhere."

"Ken, hush!"

"Okay, Daddy, see you after I have my baby. I won't be eating anymore crabs until then."

"All right, Trina. You take care now."

"I will. Thanks again."

"If I was twenty years younger, I would marry you."

Ken spoke up and said, "If you were, I would kick your ass," and walked out the store.

The man laughed at Ken.

Trina said, "Greg, he hot now."

"I know. He didn't even wait for you."

Greg and Becky got outside, and Ken was in the truck till she came out the store.

Trina smiled. "Honey, everything okay?"

"Yes dear, everything's wonderful."

"Ken, he's a nice old guy that hooks me up, so don't be mean to him. He loves my brown eyes."

"I guess he loves that big ass also?"

"Didn't ask." Trina rolled her eyes.

Back at the house.

People had started to arrive. Becky had made Kenneth a big cake and surprised him with his parents and grandparents there.

"Trina, thank you," he said, giving her a big hug and kiss.

"I need to sit down."

"You okay?"

"My stomach's a little tight. She doing a lot of moving today." Trina sat for a while eating crabs and decided to go lie on the sofa.

Chris and Val walked in the house.

Cleo said, "Hey, Ken, your friend just got here."

"Who?"

"Chris Blank."

"Oh shit."

Mitch walked in with Lisa. "Hey, everyone," he said.

Ken sat out back while Chris was talking to Trina. KJ wanted Trina.

Ken said, "Kenneth, come here. Greg, get your godson a roll and some rice, please."

"Who fixes rice at a cookout?"

"Trina and Shelly's country ass."

"Greg, you can say that again."

"Hey, Billy, go check on your daughter."

"It's your wife."

"She got company inside, and I'm playing nice like she asked me to."

His friends bust out laughing.

Chris walked out, "Hello, everyone."

Ken looked at him, got up, and walked past him. He spoke to Val and walked in the house.

"Catrina, you feeling all right?"

"Yes, Daddy."

He said, "You want some cake?"

"No, thank you." She got up, and Ken's mom said, "Trina, why you walking like that?"

"She feel like she's coming out."

"Girl, that's her pushing down. Pressure, Trina, that's all."

Lisa walked in and sat talking to Ken and Shelly.

Trina walked in her room with KJ following her. Water was gushing down her legs, and KJ looked up, watching the water run down on the floor. He said, "Potty."

"Go get Daddy, KJ, please." He sat on the step and made his way down the few steps.

Ken said, "Kenneth, come here before you fall."

"Mommy potty."

"Yes, she in the bathroom."

He kept saying, "Potty."

"Hey, Trina, you okay?"

Trina was upstairs, pushing.

Ken said, "She went to sleep. I'm kicking her ass if I'm left to entertain her ex."

"Now, now, Ken."

He went upstairs and found Trina lying on the bed, in labor and pushing.

"Shit, Trina!" He ran on the deck outside the bedroom and yelled, "Kent, get up here."

"Okay, give me a minute, bro."

"No. Now gotdamn it. Trina's having the baby." He ran up the steps from outside. "Baby, don't push. We going to the hospital."

"Ken, calm the fuck down."

"Go and get my bag out my car," Kent yelled. "I need some help up here."

Trina's mom asked, "What's going on?"

Ken ran downstairs, saying, "Trina's having the baby."

"What! We need to call her doctor."

"Mama Lena, it's too late. She's having the baby now."

Mitch said, "*Here!*"

Shelly went running and got towels and a few sheets to cover the bed.

Kent said, "Sis, I need to check you."

"Okay."

"Ken, I need that bag."

He looked. "I see her head. Trina, please don't push yet. I will tell you when. Okay? You're doing really good."

"Okay, bro, I know you got this."

Everyone was in the room.

Ken said, “Everyone to the sides. It’s bad enough my brother seen the private area.”

“Trina,” Kent said, “you’re going to feel my finger helping my niece’s head come out. She needs a little help. Becky, call 911 and tell them we need have mommy and daughter transported to the hospital. She’s being delivered right now.”

Ken paced back and forth, watching Kent deliver his daughter.

“Trina, I need a big push.”

Shelly held a light.

“One more, Trina. Ken, you ready? Because your birthday present has just arrived.”

He balled his fist, saying, “*Yes*,” as Trina lay there, tired out.

She held her baby girl as Kent cleared her airways, and they heard her soft cry.

“Welcome, Natalee.”

“Look at Naynay.”

Greg already got a name picked out. Ken held her until the ambulance got there. As the paramedics came in the room, they asked everyone to leave out, except Dad and Kent. KJ was a little scared. All he knew was Mommy had pottied and baby.

Chris was happy for Trina but was a little uneasy being there. He told Shelly, “I wonder if our baby girl would have looked like that?”

Shelly gave him a hug. “Yes.”

Trina looked at her brother-in-law, Kent, “I owe you big time.”

He just smiled.

“Bro, no, thank you so much.”

They hugged.

Ken looked at Trina, smiling, “Okay, my birthday. I will always remember my twenty-seventh birthday.”

She said, “She’s so cute. Another fly-away-hair baby.”

"Okay, Mrs. Brown, you ready to go to the hospital?"

"Yes, sir."

"Kent, you go with Trina while I get everything for her. Baby, where's your pills?"

"Everything's on the nightstand."

"I'm right behind you."

"Okay, please hurry."

Kent took the baby. They had to wrap her up in this foil-like paper to keep her warm. When they got Trina downstairs, Becky said, "Trina, I have KJ and don't worry about the room."

"Thank you," Trina replied. She could see the hurt in Chris's face.

He put his hand out, and Trina held on to it. "See you there?"

"Most definitely, Trina."

"Greg, Ken may need some help up there. He's going in circles."

His father walked upstairs to help him. "Kenneth, you good?"

"Daddy, she's really here. My baby girl is here."

"No shit, Kenneth!"

Becky had KJ and told him, "Go get toys while I help Daddy." She hurried and removed all the sheets and towels off the bed, then bagged them.

Ken said, "She has a bag packed, so he got that. Becky, anything else?"

"Her purse has all her paperwork in it."

Cleo came up. "Hey, let's go."

"Yes, while KJ's not thinking about you or Trina."

So he went down the steps.

Chris said, "Kenneth, congratulations, and I really mean that."

"Thank you, Chris."

"Fellas, you have my hotel key?"

"Yes, bro, we be over. We about to fix a plate now."

Ken and Cleo left and got over to the hospital.

Her mom said, "Baby Lee's doing good at six pounds and one ounce."

"Wow."

"Trina's blood count is low so they're working on her for a minute. Trina needed blood, and Ken had the same blood type. They had to check, then took him back."

It took a while for him to see Trina, but everyone else had seen Baby Lee. Pop-pop Billy had fell in love with his granddaughter.

"Trina did really good."

"Look at William Jones, all smiles. She melted your heart, hasn't she?"

"Yes, I think so." That damn Trina keep having these short-ass kids. Can one kid be tall like me?" Her father said. "Everybody said she marking them."

They all could finally go see Trina.

"Where's Ken at?"

"Giving blood for you."

She wished she didn't know Ken was giving blood. All she knew she was hooked up receiving blood.

"You feel okay?"

"Yes, just a little tired."

"Trina, she's beautiful."

"Oh, thank you, Chris."

"It's too bad she won't be old enough to be in my wedding."

"I know. That would have been too cute."

"February will be here before you know it, Val."

"I know, Trina. Seeing all this, I don't know about kids now."

The nurse rolled Kenneth in Trina's room, and he said, "Thank you."

His brother said, "Ken, drink the orange juice."

"Yes, sir. From now on I'll take you seriously."

"We need to talk before you leave."

Shelly was so happy she was a godmother to Baby Lee. "Anyone check on KJ?"

Greg said, "He's fine. He's helping Becky."

The nurse brought the baby in to Trina with a bottle. "Trina, you not breastfeeding?"

"Hell no! Hello Natalee, Happy Birthday."

"Let me see your eyes, Lee." Mitch said. "I like that."

Ken said, "I bet you do," and everyone laughed.

Lisa didn't catch on, so Mitch had to explain it to her.

"I never thought of it like that."

"Kent, do you want to feed your niece, your goddaughter?"

Ken asked him. "Serious, bro? I would love to do both. It's an honor to be her godfather. You know I love me some red bones." He looked at Kim, smiling.

His parents said, "Ken, she'll be in good hands with Kent."

"Trina, you have a private doctor?"

Trina's doctor walked in, and Ken said, "Look who's here."

"Yes, I'm sorry I missed everything."

"So, Doc, tell me how much it cost to deliver a baby."

"Anywhere from $13,000 to $34,000. I'm just throwing a number to you."

"Okay, so you just get paid for checking on Trina and our daughter?"

"That's correct, Kenneth."

"Okay, thanks," Trina said. "Daddy, take her. I see how you're looking at Kent. Share her, Daddy."

"For now I will."

Kenneth and Gwen both stated, "Sorry, she reminds me so much of

Trina when she was a baby. Trina look, her eyes are open....look. Awww, she has brown eyes."

Trina pulled her hat off and laughed. "Please let me put her hat back on. Bad hair day and she sucking on her finger."

"Kent, let's take a walk," Ken said to his bro.

So they walked down to the cafe and got a tea and shared a sandwich together.

"What's up?"

Ken said, "Thank you. Look, I want to apologize to you when you kept saying you wanted to open your own practice up. Now I can see your passion in bringing babies in the world."

"Thanks, big bro. That means a lot. I also want to thank you for being so hard on me about school."

"Now that you're finished, I want to do this for you. How many doctors can finish early because they're so damn smart. I mean, damn, my brother's a doctor. A gotdamn pussy doctor. I want you to come up with a plan. How much would it cost to open up your own office, pay a staff, etc.? I need everything written out, and we'll sit down with Trina and help you get started wherever you want to open an office."

"You fucking with me, right, Kenneth?"

"No, not at all."

Trina called, "Hey, can you bring me an apple juice?"

"Trina, you can't have that yet. Drink the water. I'm on my way right now."

Ken and Kent walked up, and everyone was about to leave.

Chris was holding the baby. "She's all I ever wanted."

Ken said, "Well, when you and Val are ready for practice, call us. And when Lee gets a little older, come get her." Ken looked at Trina and winked. Ken could see that losing his daughter really hurt Chris. He just put himself in Chris's place for a second, and it wasn't a good feeling to him.

"I'll take you up on that, Kenneth," Trina said. She then said good night to everyone.

Ken and Trina enjoyed their daughter all to themselves. Trina got up a little sore but didn't let that stop here from taking her shower and getting all glammed up.

Ken said, "Trina, you not going anywhere."

"Look, I need to look like something."

Ken said, "You ready make another one?"

"Kenneth, go check on our son."

Trina's dad came in the room.

"Daddy, what are you doing over here?"

"I brought you some lunch," he said. "There you go." He picked the baby up.

"Kenneth, my grandbaby looks a little better today. She was looking pale last night."

"Yes. The doctor's said her color would change."

"Daddy, what's my baby doing?"

"He's home being bossy, wanting rice and cake."

Trina said, "Let me call Becky up. He wants pancakes, Daddy."

"Look, he better start talking. All that pointing, I'm not down with. What the fuck, when you was one years old, I understood what the hell you wanted."

"No, Trina, spoiled him."

"Well, the titty belongs to someone else now. So he better get with it real quick."

Her dad asked, "Is this it?"

"Nope. We having two more babies, and then we're done," Trina said. "Ken, stop talking and get ready to go to the house. Take KJ some rice and chicken from the Chinese spot near the house, please."

So her father sat with her and his new granddaughter. She had a big mouth too. She was loud.

Her father said, "Trina, come on now. Give her the bottle."

"Daddy, she's okay. Look, you're going home, and I need to deal with her spoiled ass for what you have started."

"So just call me and I'll be there."

"Okay, Daddy."

"Hey, I'm always here no matter what, and don't you ever forget that."

"I have the coolest daddy in the whole world. Daddy, I love you. No matter how I mess up, you still treat me the same."

"Yes. You're my baby and my fuck up. Hell, Trina, you got this blood in you to look for fuck-ups to happen. Fix it or keep it moving. That's what Pop always say. And by the way Pop and Nana will be down next week."

"Okay, I can't wait."

When Ken got back, he had KJ and Trina's mom with him.

"Ken, where are your parents and grandparents?"

"Pop-pop wasn't feeling good, so they're at the house and will stopover later."

"He's okay?"

"Yes, don't you worry about Pop-pop. Billy asleep?"

"Yes, and please don't wake him or drama queen Lee up."

"What?"

"She is a drama queen, Ken. Look at her, Mom."

"Trina, what she doing?"

"She doesn't like to be changed or wiped. I need to hold her up on my breast, and she cries real loud for her bottle."

"So she's a little demanding, you telling us?"

"Yes, and Daddy wasn't helping at all, telling me to hurry up, don't let her cry."

Ken was laughing so hard. "Here's some grape juice and apple juice."

"Thanks. What, did Kent put his whole hand in my kitty? It hurts."

"You need something for the pain?"

"I had something about ten minutes ago. He was just there."

Ken sat down and had some lunch with KJ while he lay on his mommy so she could feed him. When he heard the baby, Ken went to her and said, "Kenneth, be gentle with your little sister."

He smiled at her, saying, "Baby."

"Yes, Baby Lee. Say Lee."

KJ just smiled and gave her many kisses.

Trina was feeding her, and she let KJ help hold the bottle. "Kenneth, thank you for helping Mommy with sister."

"Now come to Dad," Ken said. "Drink your juice."

"Potty, Dada."

Ken got him all squared away. He sat back in the recliner and held Kenneth until he was asleep and then he went right behind his son.

Trina said, "Ken must be tired, Mom. He didn't sleep last night. All he did was watch her sleeping."

"Really, Trina?

"Yeah."

Trina's father woke up, saying, "Key, sweetheart," to his wife.

Lena said, "You rested?"

"Yes, very much. Now what's for lunch?"

"Chicken and rice, what else?"

"Trina, come on. I hope you change your habits."

Trina finally went home that next evening, and she enjoyed her family and friends that came to visit them, but after weeks of guests, she just wanted to enjoy her kids alone. Not being rude, but she had everyone go home so she and Ken could do that. Greg and Becky was there to help when needed.

Ken was working from the house, and he told Trina he really wanted to move home with his family.

Trina just looked at him.

"Baby, come on, we have a real good thing going right now. I tell you what, I'll bring what I have at the hotel, and if things don't work out in six months, I'll get my own spot. Deal, wifey."

"Okay, deal."

Everything was going so good, but it seemed every time they went to visit the family back home, things would pop off. Because Trina had a hard time trusting Ken, every time she saw him talking to a female, she thought the worst of him. But as a woman, she knew when a bitch was trying to make moves on her man.

Trina was meeting Ken later at his club that she told him to sell soon as possible. Christine and Shelly walked in the club with Trina. Trina had got there early.

"I know that's not Kenneth kneeling down in front some female, smiling ear to ear."

Christine said, "Why would he do that? He knows, even if he wasn't doing anything, it doesn't look good for him."

"It's not going to be a good night, Shelly."

"Christine, I already know."

Trina walked over and said, "Hey, Kenneth."

He said, "Hey," stuck on stupid.

The girl looked Trina up and down, muggin her.

"Did this trick just mug me?"

"Trick bitch, who you calling a trick?"

Ken said, "Baby, come on now, we was just talking."

See, Trina had on boots so it was on.

"Get off of me," the girl yelled.

"Kenneth, we need a refill.

"Wow, so you giving drinks out?"

Trent said, "Trina, what's up?"

"Nothing much."

Then Nikki walked in. That's all she needed to see. Nikki had the nerve to sit at the table with them.

"Kenny," Nikki was yelling.

Trina, Christine, and Shelly sat down at the next table.

Christine told Trina, "Let me take my shit off right now. I see what kind of night this going to be."

A few of Trina's homegirls was in the club too. They came over and sat with them, and Ken was keeping the drinks coming at their table. But Trina wasn't drinking too much, just a little wine.

Ken said, "Trina, let's dance."

The girl yelled, "So your wife here, and you not trying to holla now."

"Trina, I wasn't trying to get with her. She was asking me about making this into a strip club."

"I told you to sell it."

"Baby, this is money. Look around. Cleo running this. I only come here, what, maybe once every two months."

Nikki kept telling the girl to chill, but the girl wouldn't listen. So after Trina and Ken danced, he walked her back to the table.

Trina's dad was in the club at the bar with his son, Timmy. He walked over and kissed Trina on the cheek.

"Hey, Kenneth, your bitch kissing a man over here."

"Did she just call you a bitch?"

Trina said, "See, every time I come out, it's a problem."

"You called my sister a bitch?"

"And if I did."

"Tramp, I'll turn this bitch out dragging your ugly ass through here."

She said, "Fuck you," and threw a drink on Timmy.

They didn't see it coming. Trina was on her ass.

"Ken, get Trina. She going off on that chick."

Ken said, "Fuck!"

Trina said, "Trick, you done lost your mind, throwing a drink in my brother's face!"

Shelly went and got Cleo, but by then her father heard Trina's loud mouth.

He said, "Why me, Lawd? Please just tell me why this damn girl can't just come out and just be nice, just once?" He told the bartender, "Hey, I'm going to need a double shot after fucking with Trina."

They laughed.

Security was trying to break the ruckus up.

Trina yelled, "Trick, you got me fucked up. This isn't about my husband. You fucking with my brother, and I kill a bitch over my blood." Trina made that known. "Fuck what you heard," looking at Nikki. She went for another round, but Ken said, "Oh no, sit down and chill out."

"I am cool, Kenneth."

"What happened over there?"

"This hoe tossed a drink in Timmy's face."

Ken walked over and talked to her. By then, Trina's blood was boiling, and she wanted Nikki's ass.

Ken came back and said, "Trina, go cool off, please."

Her father walked over and asked Trina, "Where your meds at?"

Trina wouldn't even talk to her father. She was still pissed. The girl was still mouthing off, and everyone was standing around. Trina walked over and hit that bitch dead in the face.

"I got two bastards, so I got your bastard." She beat the hell out of that chick and got a piece of Nikki's ass also. "Now tell that, Nikki."

Her father ran over and grabbed Trina up, saying, "Ken, she needs to go now before she really hurts this girl or gets locked up. Get her pills out of her bag. I need a bottle of water. Shelly, go look in my truck."

The girl went outside.

Christine said, "Bitch, if I was you, I would leave." She was still trash talking and shit.

Billy said, "Young lady, go home. If I let my daughter get on that ass, it's not going to be a good thing."

Ken told Nikki, "Go, please just go."

Her father said, "Trina, take this pill," and put it in her mouth.

By then Timmy, Cleo, and Trent had come outside.

"Trina, take the pill so you can calm down and go home to your kids."

"I don't want the damn pill." She pushed the water on her father, and it splashed all over his shirt.

That pissed him off. "Okay, so I tried the nice way. Now we're going to do it my way." He dragged her little ass out the truck, slamming her on the ground, and people were looking.

Some dude said, "Yo man, that's a female."

"Shut the fuck up or you're next." He put the pill back in her mouth and said to Shelly, "Give me the water." He held her head back by holding on to her hair. "Drink it down." He had her pinned on the ground with his knee in her chest.

Ken was like, "This is crazy. Now y'all see why I didn't want to come here tonight."

"Man, Trina will hurt a motherfucker."

"You don't say, Trent."

"Ken, I want you to take her home on Sunday and when she comes here, she doesn't come to this club. She needs to chill for a while."

"Dad, she didn't start it."

"It doesn't matter. You know this gotdamn girl's crazy, and y'all still bring her around drama. Trina, are you ready to get up now?"

"Yes," Trina said as she was coming around.

He stood her up and put her in the truck. Her dad looked at her. "Get some sleep. Ken, let her sleep as long as possible."

"Your daughter's a nut, you know that, right?"

"Yeah, I been knowing that, but did you know that?"

"A nut, no. Crazy, yes."

So Ken got Trina back at the house, and she slept that night and part of the next day. Ken had the kids with him all day.

Trina called and asked, "Where you at with my babies?"

He hung up on her. When he got back, he told her, "Don't call me with a dumbass question again. KJ, look at your hair." Ken had gotten his hair cut so nice. "You packed? We leaving 8:00 p.m. It's time to go home, Trina. You get too fucking crazy here."

"Yes. I just need to wash the kids clothes real quick."

"We'll get to it."

Timmy came in Trina's room. "Hey, sis, you okay?"

"Yes, I am."

"Trina, I love you, so please don't be fighting like that again. I know you was helping, but you have the kids now."

"I know and I promise when I come back to town. I will be good."

The kids were getting bigger. Baby Lee was now a year old, and Ken was twenty-eight years old. That year Ken took the kids to North Carolina to see his grandparents. Trina had made plans to go to a concert and then go to visit her parents, who were coming back with her.

That Friday night, Trina went to the concert with Chris and Val. They had a great time. Val's classmates were in town, so she went to the club with them after the concert. Chris and Val had pushed their wedding back to the next weekend. Chris was driving, he dropped Trina off.

Trina said, "So let me show you the programs I finally finished for Val."

"Okay, cool."

They went in, and Trina said, "Look at them. I need to get out these tight pants."

He laughed.

When she came back out she had on a sundress and said, "You want a beer?"

"No, I'm fine. You leave in the morning to see your parents?"

"Yes and I can't wait. It's been six months since I've seen them."

He pushed her hair back out her face. And Trina kissed him out of nowhere. He pulled away, and before you knew it they were on the floor getting busy. It was good to the both of them. He got up, looking at Trina and helped her up.

"Why now, Trina? I'm ready to get married in another week."

"I'm sorry."

"Trina, you're always sorry. You was sorry about lying about the baby and sorry about not caring anymore about us. Now this, Trina. That wasn't just a hit and go, that meant something to the both of us. I just felt I needed to get off my mind."

"Off your mind, huh?"

"I need to go."

Trina stood there as he walked out the door and got in his car, pulling off.

Trina went upstairs and stopped in her tracks, remembering she needed to get her shot and it was for that past Wednesday.

"Shit, shit!" she yelled. Trina went in her drawer and remembered having a plan B pill inside. She found it and took the morning-after pill.

The next day she got up and talked to KJ and Kenneth. Baby Lee was somewhere being spoiled by his grandparents. Ken asked Trina to call him when she got to her parents and she promised him no fighting if she went out.

"Husband, I love you."

"I will talk to you soon."

Trina went to her parents and had a great day with her family. They cooked out on the grill. Trina decided to go out after she talked to Ken crazy ass. Trina went into the club and had drinks from all over. She met up with Mitch, and they also had a few drinks. Lisa wasn't out that night. She had gone to some party with her girlfriends.

Mitch said, "Trina, you can't drive."

"Yes, I can."

Trina got in her truck and drove off. Mitch decided to follow her to her parents' house and make sure she got home safety. He parked and helped her in the house.

That morning Trina was feeling really bad, but she don't remember shit. She woke up in her bed under her sheet with no clothes on.

Her mother came in her room and said, "Trina, how you feeling?"

"Sick."

"Well, call Ken because he called twice for you."

"Okay," she said. "She don't even know where my phone is at."

"Someone was here with you last night."

"With me?"

"Yep, with you."

"Who?"

"Girl, I don't know."

"Timmy, come here!" Trina got up and put her robe on.

"What's up, sis?"

"Who was here with me last night?"

"I don't know. But I know you wasn't just talking."

"Oh fuck. I was messed up. I remember having drinks with Mitch, but it wouldn't be him. He's so scared of Daddy. He wouldn't come here," Trina said. "Fuck." She called Ken up and talked to him for a minute, then took a bath. She couldn't wait to get home.

That next weekend was Chris's wedding. There was a lot of tension between him and Trina. She sang at their wedding and enjoyed seeing KJ and Lee in the wedding. Val was a very pretty bride. Chris just kept looking at Trina the whole evening.

Shelly said, "Greg, something's not right. Chris and Trina have been distant all day."

"I noticed that last night at rehearsal dinner."

"I really don't want to know."

But Ken knew something wasn't right, and he wanted to find out. Trina walked past Ken, he said, "Let's dance." He kissed Trina. "What's going on with you and Chris?"

"What you talking about?"

"You two haven't said two words to each other all day."

"Nothing, Ken."

"You slept with Chris while I was away?"

"No. Now can I please go to the bathroom."

That evening before leaving, Ken and Chris went outside and Ken straight up asked him, "So how did it feel to sleep with Trina again?"

"Kenneth, it shouldn't have happened, and I told her that. She just keeps fucking my life up."

"You told Val yet?"

"Hell no!"

"Oh, now you're going into a marriage filled with lies."

"Look, I love Trina and always will, but I love my wife. I just want to move past this, okay? Ken, it will never happen again."

When Trina came out, Ken was leaning over the wall having a drink.

"Hey, you ready to go home?" he said.

"Yes."

He kissed Trina and said, "Let's get our kids and go home."

Trina and Kenneth left and told Becky and Greg that they were leaving.

"Kenneth, grab your sister's hand. Natalee, let brother hold your hand."

She pulled away.

"Little Gile, you, and your mom are my headache in life." He picked her up and said, "Stop being bossy to Kenneth."

She smiled, lying on her father's shoulder. Little brat is what Trina calls her.

Getting home, Ken didn't say a word.

In bed, he waited for Trina to lie down by him. He did his thing and got a little rough with her. Banging her hard as he could until he nutted and then he rolled over and went to sleep. He continued to be rough for months. She didn't think it could get no worse until she fell in the kitchen and Ken came running. Trina was on the floor. She was standing on a chair and fell down.

Trina kept yelling, "It's my side, Ken." She was crying.

He rushed her to the hospital.

The doctor came in, asking, "When do you have your baby?"

"What baby? I'm on the shot."

He said, "What?"

They took ultrasounds and came up with Trina being seven, going on eight months. So Ken started counting back.

"I need a blood test when she's born, Trina."

He waited outside, and she came out walking slow.

Ken got home, and he said. "Call Chris."

"Why?"

"Trina, I know all about you and him when I was away."

"Ken, it didn't mean anything."

"Trina, I'm not into the pity-party game today. Call him."

Trina called Chris, and he answered, "Yes, Trina."

"It's Kenneth. I need you here today."

"Sure, what's up?"

"Just don't bring your wife, if you want to say married."

"I'll be there in a few hours."

"So help me, Trina, if this is Chris's baby, I'm out. I'm leaving you. I will fight for my children."

When Chris got there, Trina was lying on the sofa, stomach flat, hips a little bigger, ass to die for, and breast bigger. So Ken just didn't understand.

He opened the door and said, "What's up?

"I'm here."

"Trina fell out the chair, and I had to rush her to the hospital. We found out she was seven months, almost eight months pregnant. Count back. Do the math, Chris?"

He said, "So why I'm here?"

"Tell him, Trina."

"It may be your baby. I hadn't had my shot yet, but I did take a plan B pill that same night. Look, I know it's not yours, so don't worry."

"See, this what I was talking about. You just keep fucking my life up."

"Wait, hold up one minute. Up until now, and when you fucked my wife, you wasn't thinking of fucking up your life, we're you? So until we get a blood test back, shut the fuck up."

"I'll be seeing you soon."

Ken opened the door and told Chris, "You have a nice one."

When he stepped out the door, Ken slammed the door behind him.

Trina cried, and Ken was so mad. He said, "Trina, I thought we passed all this shit, hurting each other. But I guess not. I told you I wanted a big family, but not like this, Trina."

Ken went on and on for weeks arguing.

Chris was in a bad place in his marriage. His wife left him. She wouldn't be with him if the baby was his. Trina went in the hospital to have her daughter.

She was gorgeous. Trina named her Mia Brown.

The only thing Kenneth wanted was a blood test. He called Chris and told him to get his ass to the hospital to take a blood test.

Everyone was so shocked as they did not know that Trina was pregnant. She kept it hush-hush until the baby was born.

Her parents went to the hospital when Kenneth called her parents to tell that Trina had just delivered a baby girl.

When they arrived at the hospital, her father looked at her. "Why wasn't we told about this third child?"

She broke down in tears, crying, "I messed up. I was drinking, Chris and I. Dad, it just happened."

"That's not an excuse. Why would you do this, and all the things that you've been going through with Kenneth. So now you're doing the same thing as your husband was doing."

Kenneth was so done hurt, pissed-off mad. He couldn't even look at the baby. The nurse came and got him for his blood test.

Chris arrived, and he took a blood test.

Kenneth told the lab, "I don't care how much it cost. I want this as soon as possible. I want the results back in my hands this week."

Chris looked at Trina with hate in his eyes as he walked out the hospital room after looking at the little baby girl.

A blood test finally came back the following week. The results showed that Kenneth wasn't the father, and shockingly, Chris wasn't also the father.

Trina was lying on the bed as she just finished feeding her daughter.

Kenneth walked upstairs and charged at Trina. He grabbed her by the throat and said, "Bitch, who have you been with? She's not mine, it's not Chris's, so whose baby is it? Who the fuck was you with?"

Trina was gasping for air, turning blue. He looked at the baby and let her go.

"Start talking, Catrina, *today.*"

"I haven't been with anyone else. I'm telling you the truth." She rambled on, saying she went out one time and had drinks with Mitch. "I don't know, I can't remember. I was drunk, Kenneth. I remember the next morning with a hangover, waking up with no clothes on under the sheets. And I remember my brother asking me who was with me last night, and I said nobody."

Kenneth said, "Wait one fucking minute. You was out drinking with Mitch. You can't remember nothing—how fucking stupid do you sound."

"I'm telling you I don't remember anything. I didn't sleep with anybody. I was drunk, passed out."

Kenneth left, pissed. He drove around, and then he thought that Mitch has been in love with Trina for years, have been trying to be with his wife on the down low. He went on a rampage. He went speeding over to Mitch's house and knocked on the door. No one answered. He knocked again.

Lisa answered the door. Lisa said, "Hey, Kenneth, what can I do for you?"

"I need to speak to your husband."

"Sure, he's down in the basement working out. Go ahead down."

Kenneth walked down in the basement.

Mitch smiled at him as he walked in, saying, "Hey, what's up, Mr. Brown."

Not a word from Ken. He just charged at Mitch and pinned him into the wall and said, "Motherfucker, you fucking my wife."

Mitch looked ten carats stupid, asking, "What are you talking about?"

"Oh, I think you know what I'm talking about. You and my wife, out drinking one night. She get fucked up and you're going to tell me the rest."

Mitch said, "Look, it didn't supposed to happen that way. She was flirting with me all night. She was drunk, dude, I know. So was I. Look I followed her to her parents' house and made sure she got in the house. She got upstairs. She fell on the bed and started taking her clothes off, and it just happened."

"So she fell on the bed, Mitch? She was drunk. You took my wife's body from her while she was drunk, motherfucker."

"Kenneth, she knew it was me. We both were fucked up."

"Don't even use that as an excuse."

"Trina kept on saying my name over and over, so she knew it was me, man, come on."

Ken punched Mitch in the face and started beating him like a bitch on the street.

Lisa came running downstairs, screaming and yelling, "Stop, stop, you're hurting my husband."

Kenneth let him go and stood up. "Okay, Lisa, I'll stop. Maybe you'll get the balls to beat his ass one time—it's overdue—when I tell you what he has done and what he has now."

"What's Kenneth talking about, Mitch?"

"You may want to sit down for this one. Mrs. Lee." He looked at Mitch. "Trina just had a baby last week. I was away when this child was conceived, and I thought it was Chris's baby, so we did a blood test. She's not mine, and she's not Chris. Then Trina told me about her little night on the town with your husband, getting off shit face. So I put two and two together, so that's why I'm here. Mitch has a little girl by my wife. Her name is Mia. Do you hear that, Lisa, Mitch…Mia Mitch…Mia. Sound pretty cute, doesn't it, Mr. Casanova? So now I'm going to tell you, you're going to take your little sneaky, conniving ass to get a blood test, and if it's yours, I'm fucking you up on sight. Now you have a nice day." When he was walking out, he said, "Mitch, blood test. ASAP. Time is ticking."

Lisa said, "Is this true, Mitchell?"

"Yes."

She walked away, saying, "I can't do this anymore."

He yelled, "For better or worse, Lisa. Remember your vows. Hey, it's not like I was flaunting that mistress."

The result came in. Mia was 99.9 percent Mitch's daughter.

Teaser for the next book coming soon

Kenneth got the news, and that Friday evening, he waited as Mitch pulled into the gym parking lot and hit the gas, running into his truck.

He said, "Get out. I told you if she was yours, I owe you a beatdown. Lights out, motherfucker."

All you could hear was screaming.

"Nooooooo!"

CPSIA information can be obtained
at www.ICGtesting.com
Printed in the USA
LVHW031022171121
703472LV00020B/963

9 781637 287835